THE ORPHAN
AND
INCARNATION

THE ORPHAN AND INCARNATION

Ajay Mohapatra

Translated by

Manoranjan Mishra

Black Eagle Books
2022

Black Eagle Books
USA address:
7464 Wisdom Lane
Dublin, OH 43016

India address:
E/312, Trident Galaxy, Kalinga Nagar,
Bhubaneswar-751003, Odisha, India

E-mail: info@blackeaglebooks.org
Website: www.blackeaglebooks.org

First International Edition Published by
Black Eagle Books, 2022

THE ORPHAN AND INCARNATION
by **Ajay Mohapatra**
Email ID: ajaykmohapatra@gmail.com

Translated by **Manoranjan Mishra**

Cover : **Sushil Puhan**
Interior Design: Ezy's Publication

ISBN- 978-1-64560-242-2 (Paperback)
Library of Congress Control Number: 2022930047

Printed in the United States of America

Translator's Note

Ajay Mohapatra's latest book presents two novellas—*The Orphan and Incarnation*, originally published in Odia in 2021.

The first novel *The Orphan* centres round Pranakrushna, Padmabati, Sridhar and Sambhabana. Being issueless for many years after marriage, Pranakrushna adopts a son. Later when a girl-child is born to him and Padmabati, he leaves it under the care of Mr. Joseph Albert, the owner of a Children's Home and an Orphanage. This he does apprehending that Padmabati's love for the adopted child might diminish at the sight of her own child and the child might be compelled to live an orphaned life. He keeps the entire episode under wraps. The boy, Sridhar grows up to become an Engineer in London. He marries Sambhabana. Pranakrushna sells the paternal property in his village and donates the entire eighty lakh rupees to the orphanage. A greedy and selfish Sambhabana ill-treats her mother-in-law after Pranakrushna's death for not getting a share in the property. In a strange turn of events, it is revealed by Mr. Albert that Sridhar was the orphaned child and he got a new lease of life because of Pranakrushna. The story has a beautiful twist at the end.

The second novel *Incarnation* centres round Manashi-- a haughty, fashionable and modern woman, and Piyush, a country lad. Both of them, though possess contrary characters, are drawn into a live-in relationship. For Manashi, her womb is a machine that can be turned on and turned off at will. Gratification of sensual desire is her sole purpose in life. Consequently, she gets pregnant quite frequently. After having aborted twice, she gets pregnant for a third time. The doctor tells her that she might not become a mother in future if she went ahead with another abortion. This compels her to go for marriage with Piyush, much to the dismay of her wealthy and fashionable parents. Despite the initial hardships, they get married. It is only then Manashi realizes the importance of a husband. She now learns that husbands are soul-mates and not playboys.

The story has a twist. Piyush's mother Suhasini conceives a child only a couple of months before the former's marriage. Piyush feels offended at this unexpected development. He deserts his parents and leaves his village. Then the second twist starts in the story. The twists are sure to keep the readers absorbed.

The two novels highlight two burning problems that the society faces today—ill-treatment of in-laws in the hands of their daughter-in-law and live-in relationship.

On the occasion of the publication of the book, I thank Mr. Ajay Mohapatra for entrusting the task of translating the novels to me.

I also express my deep sense of gratitude to Mr. Satya Patnaik, Director, Black Eagle Books for publishing this book.

Manoranjan Mishra

CONTENTS

THE ORPHAN

One

Pranakrushna Kar is renowned among his friends and colleagues for being a very amiable person. He started his career as an S.O in the Secretariat and was subsequently promoted to the post of Joint Secretary before retiring from service four years ago. He is a native of Marshaghai of Kendrapada District. His wife, Padmavati, is a native of Kendrapada town. She is two years younger than her husband. Pranakrushna is around sixty-four now. Both of them celebrate their birthday in the month of December. Padmavati is better known among her friends and acquaintances as Padma, the name by which her husband Pranakrushna also loves to address her. The couple share an intimate relationship. They love each other deeply bound by a profound mutual faith. No one has ever seen any domestic squabbles affecting their relationship. If Pranakrushna took a decision and conveyed it to her, she would blindly accept it. She would always think, "If he has taken the decision, he must have weighed its pros and cons and it must be right." Such a deep understanding has helped them wade across the stormy waters of life during their twenty-eight years of togetherness, without any jerk. Padma would leave all the decisions regarding her life in the hands of her husband for she placed as much faith in him as much she did in God. Not an iota of faith more or less!

Pranakrushna invested his entire earning in the

education of his son, Sridhar. He now works as a Software Engineer. These days he lives in London with his family. Pranakrushna owns a small house in the Laxmisagar area of Bhubaneswar, allotted in his name by the Housing Board. It's a one-storeyed small building. What more an honest person could have achieved in his life? Despite the occasional weal and woe, he had spent most part of his life quite happily with his wife. However, his world changed since the day he was detected with cancer, that too in an advanced stage. He has become bed-ridden since then. The bed has become his world. This had disheartened the couple. Padma suffered from chronic back pain. Besides, pain in the knee and joints added to her discomfiture. Normal movement had become cumbersome for her. Despite her illness, she had to take care of her bed-ridden husband, and carry out household chores like cooking and cleaning. The domestic help would visit only in the morning. She would sweep the rooms and wash the utensils. Padma would often feel lonely. She craved to meet son Sridhar, daughter-in-law Sambhabana, and granddaughter Riya. She had not met Riya even once, although she had seen her photo only. She had completed four in the meantime. After completing B.Tech from KIIT, Sridhar was selected to join a Bangalore based company through campus placement. After working there for two years, he left for London. Pranakrushna arranged his marriage with Sambhabana, the only daughter of Dhirendra Tripathy. An extremely beautiful girl, Sambhabana was also a software engineer. Sridhar fell in love with her at first sight and agreed to the proposal. Pranakrushna had to ready all arrangements. Sridhar reached from London only for a week. The marriage was solemnized with great pomp and ceremony. The newly-wed couple left for London thereafter.

Two

Sambhabana was the only daughter of Dhirendra. He had brought her up with great love and care. After she was married off, the couple felt very lonely. The same was the case with Pranakrushna. After the departure of his son and daughter-in-law, he and his wife also felt lonely. Such things have become quite common in most households these days. Only a person who lives alone can experience how distressing loneliness is. Pranakrushna and Padmavati are going through such experiences at the moment.

After a few days of Sridhar and Sambhabana's marriage, the former's mother-in-law passed away. He arrived in India with his wife only for five days. The couple visited Jajpur for the death rituals. After the rituals were over, they visited Bhubaneswar. This was only for a couple of hours. On the same day they left for London. The following year, Sridhar's father-in-law passed away in heart attack. The couple visited India for ten days. On the day of their return, they stayed at Bhubaneswar only for a couple of hours. Padma felt angry and hurt but her husband advised her not to make an issue of it. She was a sort of woman who never disregarded her husband's advice. Rather, she considered her husband her God and his advice, sacrosanct. Happiness of her husband was her prime concern. Pranakrushna would always advise her, thus:

"Why do you consider Sambhabana your daughter-in-law? Why don't you consider her your daughter? Doesn't her happiness bring us pleasure?"

Padmabati would melt like a burning candle. She, who always craved for a daughter, would be filled with affection and warm feelings. Pranakrushna never had to strive hard to pacify her. This emotional exploitation always worked. After pranakrushna was detected with cancer, his son and daughter-in-law had not even met him once. They talked with him, as a matter of routine, only on weekends. The old couple would wait eagerly for a call from their son. On some occasions, it wouldn't come at all. Pranakrushna kept his feelings hidden; he never reacted openly. Padmabati would feel upset with their son's indifference. At times, she would say,

"My son never behaved with me like that. He was extremely obedient."

"Haven't you seen that?"

"Did he ever remain away from me for long? How deeply he loved me? It's only after marriage that he has undergone a change."

Pranakrushna would smile within. He would keep gazing at her face surreptiously. He would visualize the innocent and simple soul within.

At times, Padmabati would feel vexed. She would remark, "Everybody cautioned us not to go ahead with a bride from Jajpur. I couldn't say 'no' as you were interested in the proposal. However, I was always very apprehensive. Now we have to face the music."

Pranakrushna would flash a smile. He would repeat his oft-repeated dialogue, "Don't consider Sambhabana as your daughter-in-law. Take her for your daughter."

"If you consider her your daughter, how can she be ill-famed for being a resident of Jajpur."

"She will be someone either from Kendrapara or Bhubaneswar."

Padmabati wouldn't drag the arguments any further. She would flash a smile and say, "No one would match you in arguments. You may say whatever you wish but I can't help being apprehensive."

"What a calm, quiet and simple child our son is! Sambhabana is lucky to have got him as her husband. This is the result of good deeds of her past birth."

"Pranakrushna would listen to Padmabati with care. The praise of Sridhar would fill his body and soul with delight. He would feel enchanted for a moment. Visions of Sridhar's childhood would flash before him. He would gaze at Padmabati in eyes brimming with tears. Beaminging enchantingly, he would repeat his favourite dialogue with ease, "Consider her your daughter. Only then all your problems will be solved."

"I consider her not as my daughter-in-law but as my daughter. You can see; I'm extremely relaxed."

"Once you take her as your daughter, you'll feel relaxed like me."

"Her happiness will fill us with delight."

"What else do we expect at this age?"

"If our son and daughter-in-law settle down in London happily, it will certainly be a matter of great delight for us. What more do we need?"

Despite her husband's inspiring words, Padmabati found it difficult to accept Sambhabana as her daughter. From some corner of her heart a voice rose reminding her again and again that she was her daughter-in-law and not daughter. The expectations of a mother-in-law always took over. She believed that if her son had changed, it was because of Sambhabana. Matters became complicated as they hadn't met each other even once during the last five years.

Five years ago, Sridhar justified his inability to visit them by claiming that Sambhabana was pregnant. After Riya was born, he claimed that she was too small to travel. After Riya had turned three Padmabati demanded that they should visit India but in vain. Sridhar at that time said, "Sambhabana is preparing for a new job. Hence, it won't be possible for them to visit India."

Then he said, "Sambhabana has a new job. How would she go on leave now? She needs some time to settle down. Perhaps you won't understand."

Padmabati felt hurt when Sridhar didn't arrive for two years even after learning that his father had been diagnosed with cancer. She was filled with anger and disenchantment for him. She was now certain that her son behaved so irresponsibly only because of his wife. This compelled her not to accept her as her daughter. She writhed in agony. Since it was not possible to share her disenchantment with anyone, she would silently shed tears. She would take Sridhar's childhood photos in her lap, embrace it and shed copious tears.

Three

Padmabati always mused over the past. She would remind herself of Sridhar's childhood days and whine. One day, Padmabati suddenly came across an old photograph of Sridhar in an album. He was a one year of old toddler then. He was very tiny when he was brought home. Her eyes welled up in tears when the incidents related to those days flashed before her.

Padmabati was about twenty-two years of age. She had passed her I.A. and was enrolled in Kendrapara College for her B.A. degree. Her family received proposal from Pranakrushna's family for marriage. Without wasting any more time, her parents arranged her marriage. Pranakrushna had just been employed. He was around twenty-five then. He shifted to Bhubaneswar with his new bride. The government quarter allotted to him had two bedrooms and a drawing room, besides a dining room. At the back, there was the kitchen with an attached toilet. Another toilet for common use stood some distance away. The quarter had facility for twenty-four-hour water supply. Padma brought her father and mother-in-law to stay with them. She took care of them heartily and with all sincerity. The old couple was extremely delighted to have got such a loving and caring daughter-in-law. They treated her as their daughter. How fast those blissful days passed!

Four

Pranakrushna was the only child of his parents. It was but natural for the old parents to insist on him to go for a child as soon as possible. Unfortunately, Pranakrushna and Padma didn't have a child during five years of their marriage. On a couple of occasions, Padma had miscarriages. The couple consulted doctors; they beseeched God to bless them with a child. However, their prayers went unheard. In the meantime, Pranakrushna's father passed away before being blessed with grand-fatherhood. The unfortunate condition might have engendered sour feelings in him but he never expressed those. He never considered Padma any inferior to his daughter. Every time Padma had a miscarriage, she would feel disheartened. Her father-in-law would console her saying, "Daughter, don't feel disheartened. One day or the other, I shall return to your lap as your son. God can never be unkind to one like you."

At the words of her father-in-law, tears would well up in Padma's eyes. Her loving mother-in-law would arrive and wipe away her tears. She would say, "Don't lose hope. Wait and see. I'll return to you as your daughter-in-law. I shall pay off your debt by serving you the way you have done to us."

Padma thought she was fortunate to have been blessed with such parents-in-laws. She treated them not only like her own parents but worshipped them like God. It's true that her father-in-law wanted a child as heir to the family but he didn't feel completely disheartened. The reason was that he basked in the love, care and affection of Padma. He always considered himself her child. He didn't wish to leave the world and go away, deserting her.

Unfortunately, Padma lost her mother-in-law the year following her father-in-law's death. An emptiness reigned in the entire house. Padma felt as if she had lost her two children. She felt lonely. Mentally, she felt weak and exhausted.

Five

Twelve years had passed in the meantime. One morning, Pranakrushna was reading the calendar and murmuring something. He spoke in a gentle voice, "Padma, will you please accede to a request of mine?"

Padma looked at her husband in eyes of wonder. After a moment of silence, she looked unblinkingly into his face and said, "Have I ever disregarded you or ever had an opinion contrary to yours? If not, why are you seeking my opinion?"

After a brief pause, she added, "Do whatever you consider right for us. I have no objections to make."

Pranakrushna said, "It's high time we adopted a child."

Padma had perhaps harboured such a thought, just after the death of her father and mother-in-law. For some obscure reason, she had not been able to disclose her heart to her husband. A new sun started rising in her. Like a sunflower turning automatically in the direction of the rising sun, she turned her head towards her husband. Her face appeared charming and bright like a freshly-bloomed flower. Like the soft golden rays of the morning sun, the smile that emanated from within added glow to her face. With a sense of pleasure, she said, "Yes. It would be very nice. I feel very lonely after you leave for office. Most of the time, I feel desperate. With a child around, things will change."

Six

Once the decision was made, Pranakrushna paid visits to many orphanages. During the course of one such visit, he came across a Christian Missionary and manager of St. Joseph Orphanage, Joseph Albert Ekka. With the passage of time intimacy between the two grew. Pranakrushna was deeply touched by the latter's sincerity, honesty and principles. He made it a point to donate regularly to the orphanage. He would also make some time regularly to visit the place. He fell in love with the place and its inmates.

Pranakrushna never had any discussions with Reverend Ekka about his problems. He thought he should rather wait for an opportune moment. Padma was in greater need of a child. One morning, he received a call from Reverend Ekka on his land phone. He picked up the receiver and said 'Hello'. Reverend Ekka didn't say much. He only spoke briefly.

"Can we meet immediately?"

Pranakrushna didn't enquire where he wished to meet him as he knew quite well that he met people only at the orphanage. In reply he only said, "Yes, I'm reaching you very soon."

He got ready to go. The bunch of motorcycle keys was hanging from a nail on the wall. He took it. He collected his helmet from the shelf too. Padmavati emerged from the bedroom, all ready. It was Janmasthami, the holy birthday of Lord Krishna. She thought her husband was ready to take her to the temple. At the sight of her husband, she said, "We are going to the temple. Why haven't you changed your clothes? Where are you heading at this hour?"

Pranakrushna replied, "I just remembered something urgent. We are surely going to the temple. I know it's the birthday of Lord Krishna. I'll come back soon."

Padma knew very well what stuff her husband was made of. She had deep faith in him. She knew that he would surely take him for a darshan of the lord at the temple, no matter how late he returned. She didn't change her clothes anymore. Placing the *bhog* basket on the shelf, she waited patiently for him to return.

Seven

Pranakrushna proceeded straight in the direction of the orphanage. Although his intimacy with Reverend Albert had grown over the last few days, he was skeptical about the purpose of the latter's untimely summon so early in the morning. He reached the orphanage soon. He was ushered in to the room of Reverend Albert, who was eagerly waiting for him. Pranakrushna appeared a little anxious. With a great deal of uncertainty clouding his mind, he asked, "Sir, is everything fine?"

Reverend Albert replied, "Yes, everything is fine. Please have a seat. Feel at ease. There is not much trouble."

Pranakrushna's mind was troubled by a dilemma. The words of Reverend Albert reassured him. He felt relaxed. Reverend Albert ordered a glass of water for Pranakrushna. He offered him the glass and spoke with a smile, "Lord Krishna has taken birth in our orphanage today."

Pranakrushna failed to decipher what exactly he was hinting at. With the dilemma still reigning his mind, he looked in his direction. Reverend Albert passed some hints to an attendant standing nearby. The attendant understood the hint clearly. Carrying a one-year-old baby in her lap, she returned to the room. The cries of the baby soon filled the room. A very charming baby! It had a fair complexion, sharp nose, chubby cheeks, and big round eyes. Its head and cheek were adorned with dabs of kajal. It wore a yellow dress and yellow knickers. A locket of Lord Hanuman tied to a black thread hung around its neck. The appearance of the innocent child and its enchanting smile were bewitching enough to melt the heart of the cruelest person. Pranakrushna was but a humane and compassionate individual. How could he resist the child's attraction? He took the child to his lap and showered his love on it. Surprisingly, the child stopped crying. He gave out a faint smile instead. Reverend Albert said, "Someone left the child on our verandah last night at about two o' clock amidst incessant rain. Attracted by its cries, I went out and discovered it. Coincidentally, today is the birthday of Lord Krishna."

Pranakrushna understood explicitly what he was hinting at. Reverend Albert didn't stop there. He continued further, "I somehow feel I should not keep this Krishna in my orphanage and see him grow as an orphan. This is exactly why I rang you up so early in the morning."

Pranakrushna felt extremely delighted. He understood the hint of Reverend Albert. How would he express his gratitude? Words betrayed him. He remained mum for a moment. With his eyes welling up in tears, he said, "Sir, today I feel that Lord Jesus can comprehend the sorrows of Hindus. I am short of words to express my thankfulness to you."

Streams of happy tears ran down from Pranakrushna's eyes. Reverend Albert got up from his seat and patted him on his back. He walked to the gate to see him off.

Eight

Padmabati was waiting in the drawing room for her husband's return. The cries of the child at the door startled her. She ran towards the door and looked at her husband in wonder. She failed to understand where her husband had picked the child from. Awestruck, she looked at her husband for a moment once again. She was waiting for a darshan of Lord Krishna on the occasion of Janmashtami but lo- the Balkrishna was already there in front of her. Lord Krishna had taken incarnation and appeared in front of her. She no more went to the temple. She engaged herself in the service of Him. Intense delight filled Padma's mind. She was engrossed by a divine experience. She felt as if lightning shot through her mind and body. She experienced a strange sensation of love for the child.

She bathed the child and dressed him in a new dress. She hung a gold locket around his neck. She applied talcum powder and drew a kajal mark on his head. She took the dress the child had worn and the lead Hanuman locket, kept these in a tin box, and locked it carefully. She hugged the box as if it contained her heart. She paid obeisance to lord Hanuman. She felt as if it was not a mere Hanuman locket but the real Lord Hanuman stood in front of her. She had deep faith in God. The incident that had happened unexpectedly not only elated her but also reinforced her faith in God.

She returned to the drawing room, handed over the child to her husband, and said, "This is my Kanha."

The child had by then become Pranakrushna's darling. He saw a strange gleam in his wife's eyes. There was a delightful smile playing on her lips. For the last several years, she had lost it somewhere. It was as if the cursed stream had released itself from the curse and had started flowing perennially, brimming with water. For a very long time, he had been earnestly praying God to bless him with such a happy family.

Since the child had come to her on the birthday of Lord Krishna, she fondly named it Kanha. That evening, a feast was arranged. Cakes were cut. The child was christened 'Sridhar'. Since that day Padmabati had carefully placed the child in the inner recesses of her heart, just as the old witch of the legends had hidden the prince in a box under seven fathom deep mud. Sridhar had become her heart, her life and her world. Sridhar, on his part, never stayed away from his mother even for a day. He sought his mother's advice in all matters. His neighbours and friends teased him and called him an effeminate. The problem hardly found a solution till the day he passed from KIIT University. Even when he was selected for a job at Bangalore, after completion of his engineering degree, he insisted on not going there without his mother. Pranakrushna was compelled to accompany him with his wife. They returned to Bhubaneswar with his wife only all arrangements for his stay there were satisfactorily made. When the time for the return came, the mother-son duo cried so bitterly that a crowd gathered to witness what the problem was. On realizing what the matter was, some of them burst into laughter whereas some others praised them saying, "It feels great to learn that such mothers and sons exist even today." The love that existed between the two was in no way inferior to the love that existed between Sri Krishna and Yashoda.

Times had changed. In the meantime, Sridhar had become a professional. He had got married and had a family. The string of love between him and his mother was snapped. 'Time' had acquired a new significance for him. He needed a handsome bank balance. He wished three things besides others—promotion, citizenship in London and his own palatial building. In comparison to these, the worth of mother's love had diminished.

Nine

Padmabati craved for the presence of Sridhar. During old age, illness or infirmity one seeks support and sympathy. The presence of a son by bedside during such occasions enlivens one. Padma felt sad as her son lived far away. He rang up only once a week. However, thinking that her tears might bode ill, she stopped shedding tears, put Sridhar's old photo carefully back in the old trunk and locked it.

She accompanied Pranakrushna for a checkup at the doctor. Doctor Senapati, without any hesitation, remarked that the patient's condition had deteriorated further and that he was in his last stage.

Pranakrushna was supposed to remain alive for another fifteen or twenty days.

Padma felt disoriented. She felt so terribly lost that she hardly realized when the car had covered the distance between Cuttack and Bhubaneswar. She felt like ringing up to Sridhar and passing him the message. She rang up twice. On both the occasions, Sambhabana picked up the phone. Padma hang up saying that she would talk to Sridhar later. For some obscure reason, she didn't feel like revealing anything to her. When he didn't call back for a long time, she decided to ring him up. This time Sridhar received the call. Padmabati's bund of patience breached.

All anger and disappointments flowed away in tears. She sobbed uncontrollably.

Sridhar was working on the laptop with the Bluetooth device stuck into his ears. The emotional outbursts of his mother stopped at the threshold of his ears; they failed to penetrate into his heart. Lost into the task at hand, he spoke without a care,

"Hmm."

"Say what you want."

"Speak briefly."

"I am very busy now."

It was strange how the bewildered cries of his mother failed to penetrate into his heart and create a stir. Padmabati reined in her emotions and said,

"Kahna!"

"We are going to lose your father very soon."

"Doctor says he is going to live at best for fifteen to twenty days."

Sridhar spoke as if he had lost his cool.

"Do you think doctors are gods?"

"How can they predict how long father is going to live?"

"Why do you believe what they say?"

"Let the treatment continue as it is."

"I will reach at the appropriate hour."

Sridhar didn't have time either to continue the conversation or to enquire into his father's illness in detail. Padma wished that Sridhar should talk with her longer, discuss their weal and woe in great detail, and reassure her with his soothing words. However, nothing of that sort happened. Sridhar spoke in a professional manner and confined his conversation to a few words. How would Padma put up with such behavior? She broke into sobs once again and placed the receiver down. Her sobs reached Pranakrushna's ears in the other room. He spoke in a faint voice,"Why are you crying, Padma?"

"No one has any control over death--neither I nor you or Sridhar."

"What can he do if he reaches India early?"

Wiping her tears with the end corner of her saree, Padma said,

"Kanha has changed much."

"He has no time to talk with me."

"He hardly has any faith in me."

"Did he ever behave like this earlier?"

"Just think how he behaved in Bangalore."

"Don't you remember how he broke down when the parting moments came? How the residents of the colony gathered in wonder!"

The incidents flashed before Pranakrushna's inner eyes one by one. He however remained mum and responded only with 'Hmm'. Padma broke into sobs once again and said,

"No…Kanha was never so heartless."

"He has greatly changed under the influence of Sambhabana."

"How conveniently a son forgot his parents under the influence of his wife!"

Ten

Pranakrushna's condition deteriorated day by day. Padmabati helplessly counted days. Each day passed like an aeon. She had no regular hours for eating, drinking or sleeping. She would sit, throughout the day and night, beside her husband's bed. Pranakrushna took liquids and saline in diet. A nurse visited them twice a day. She would leave after her duty was over. During exigencies, a doctor would visit them. When he came for checkup the last time, he told, "There is no need of any further checkup. Please give up any hope of recovery. However, the nurse would come on regular visits."Besides Pranakrushna, Kanha was theonly person in whom Padmabati reposed confidence. She felt very helpless now. The surroundings appeared bleak. What would she do after her husband passed away? The worries shattered her mentally. Tears would refuse to stop rolling down her eyes. She would try not to shed tears in her husband's presence but tears defied her at times.

After about five days, Sridhar rang up from London. Padmabati picked up the receiver and said, "Hello."

Sridhar said, "Mama!"

Padmavati felt surprised. She thought, "It is not Sunday today…not even a holiday. Has Kanha really changed? Is he really worried about his father and mother?"

Sridhar said, "Mama!"

"Don't you worry at all."

"We are reaching India very soon."

In a moment, Padmabati felt relaxed.

The sound of 'Mama' filled her with courage and delight. The gentle Padmabati spoke up,

"Yes, my dear…reach as soon as possible."

"Your father is seeking for you."

Before Padmabati could finish, Sridhar's voice was heard,

"Listen Mama…I am very busy here. Perhaps you won't understand."

"Only for the sake of father, I have applied for leave."

"Are you telling the truth?"

Padmabati found herself facing a great dilemma. She asked confusedly, "Kanha, what are you talking about?"

Without any hesitation or concern for her feelings, the heartless Sridhar spoke,

"Don't you understand what I am going to ask you about?"

: Obviously about father's death.

: You informed me four days ago that father was going to survive for another fifteen or twenty days.

: We are extremely worried about that.

: Sambhabana also had great faith in your words. She urged we should immediately reach there.

:That's why we are going on leave.

Padma couldn't say anything in reply. From her wailing, Sridhar concluded that whatever he had heard was true. He hung up. Sridhar's words tortured the innocent and simple-minded Padma. What could be more reassuring for her than the fact that her son and daughter-in-law were reaching very soon? She could deal with the trouble more confidently if her children stood by her. She conveyed the happy news to her husband. Pranakrushna gave a faint smile with his lips pressed against each other. The smile was not aimed at his son but his innocent wife. He thought that when Sridhar returned, he would take care of Padma. If it so happened, he could die a peaceful death. This was precisely why God had left Sridhar in his hands.

Eleven

Since the day Padma had received the message from Sridhar that he was coming back to India to be by her side at this time of distress, she had grown restive. She felt mentally stronger. She felt reassured. These days, she frequently looked outside the gate. If there was some sound, she would rush to the front verandah. She felt as if Sridhar had arrived.

Sridhar reached five days after he had rung up. He was accompanied by Sambhabana and Riya. Padma was pleasantly surprised as her granddaughter appeared like an exotic doll. Sambhabana had warned Riya beforehand not to unnecessarily gel with others. The child wished to gel well with others and play with them but fear for mother restrained her.

Sridhar and Sambhabana reached the door of the room in which Pranakrushna lived. They stood near the door, said 'namaskar' to him, asked after his health, and left for their bedroom. Pranakrushna had got a bedroom constructed with attached bath and latrine, exclusively for Sridhar. He had spent quite a sum in creating all facilities there. However, it was not much to the liking of Sridhar or Sambhabana. Sridhar had expressed his displeasure quite openly with Pranakrushna. Although Pranakrushna felt a little hurt, he didn't say anything to his son. The husband and wife duo stayed in that bedroom. Of course, Sridhar had permitted Sambhabana to stay in a hotel room if she wished but the couple decided to stay at home thinking that the neighbours might criticize their action.

Throughout the day, the couple would keep themselves confined to the bedroom. They would work on their computers from its confines. Padma would serve them food there. She had to make all arrangements starting from their coffee to breakfast, lunch and dinner. At times, they would order food from the hotels. The child had a computer and a number of computer games to give her company. She hardly took any interest in others. Their life was hardly different from the lives they spent at London. Only Padma's responsibilities had multiplied. Despite her engagements in the kitchen, she was happy. What delighted her was the fact that her children spent their days right in her company. Like a foolish woman, she would at times ask some questions to her son:

"Kanha, please tell me one thing. What keeps you so busy? Why do you slog throughout the day and night? Your father never worked so hard."

Sridhar would burst out to a smile and say, "Times have changed. You won't understand. These days we work from home."

Padma would retort, "During the thirty-five years your father worked, he hardly did any office work at home. Why are you doing it then?"

Sriddhar remarked, "The world has undergone vast changes, mother. He hardly knows anything about computers. He has become obsolete. Such people are not even fit for a peon's job in our company."

Padma fell silent. When the proposal for marriage was received, she had just completed her intermediate classes and joined the undergraduate classes in a college near their village. Pranakrushna was a graduate. She was very proud that she and her husband were counted amongst the educated. Sridhar's words compelled her to think that she and her husband were really uneducated.

Twelve

Sridhar and Sambhabana would, in a matter of routine, wish Pranakrushna good morning and good night. Their responsibilities for him were confined only to this. In fact, they were not interested in telling him good morning and good night; they rather wanted to confirm if his condition was deteriorating and if he was going to leave for his heavenly abode just as the doctor had predicted. If there was a delay, all their plans would go topsy-turvy. Keeping the expected date of obsequies rituals in mind, they had booked their flight tickets. They had only five extra days in hand. It was not possible to get leave beyond what they had been allowed.

Sambhabana would often feel vexed with the Indian doctors. She would say, "One should never bank on the prediction of Indian doctors. He was expected to live for fifteen days only. Fifteen days have passed in the meantime but there has not been any significant deterioration in his health."

Like a hen-pecked husband, Sridhar would echo Sammbhabana's feelings:

'Yes, I also have the same views. One can never have any faith in the predictions of Indian doctors."

Padma, however, would sit beside the bed of her

husband throughout the night. She would pray God to grant her husband more years to live. One day added to her husband's life was like an aeon for her. That would provide her an opportunity to spend an extra day in the company of her husband. How would Sridhar and Sambhabana understand the worth of such love and affection? Their eyes only had dreams of London. London was like heaven for them. Earning money was the be-all and end-all of their lives. When the cataract of money blurs one's vision, one hardly measures the worth of love, affection, fellow-feeling, and relationship. The same thing had happened with Sridhar and Sambhabana.

Thirteen

The following day, an acquaintance from Pranakrushna's native place visited him. In his childhood, Sridhar addressed him as Chaini uncle. He was in charge of all their property including their agricultural land, mango groves, fish ponds, bamboo clusters and cashew plantations. Pranakrushna was the only child of his parents. He didn't even have a sister. Since Pranakrushna lived in the city he didn't have the time to take care of all the property.

While discussing the weal and woe with Sridhar, he said, "I advised your father many times not to dispose of the paternal property that he had inherited from his forefathers. He gave my advice a damn. He disposed those of one by one. The homestead land was the only property that was left; he got it registered in my name. He didn't demand a single penny from me. Now, your family is left with no landed property in the village.

What could be her father-in-law's intention behind all these? Sambhabana found the question perplexing.

"Uncle, how much money would he have got from the sale of the property?"

Chaini in fact didn't have any correct information. He made some calculations with his fingers and came out with a figure. "The amount must be between forty to fifty lakh rupees." He sold everything for a song. Had he bargained a little, he could have easily earned about eighty lakh rupees, or even more.

A strange thought came to Sridhar and Sambhabana's mind. They had been eagerly waiting for Pranakrushna's death. Now they wanted him to confess where he had parked the money or how he had spent such a huge amount.

Without any further delay, Sridhar held a discussion with Padmabati that evening:

"Mother! Is it true that father has disposed of all the landed property?"

In a gentle, unperturbed and soft voice Padmabati replied, "Yes, that's true. I heard about it from Chaini just now."

Sridhar found it difficult to buy his mother's argument. Sambhabana, who was sitting beside her husband, was certain that her mother-in-law was only trying to put a veil on the entire affair. Sridhar continued, "Chaini uncle informed me that the sale had fetched father about forty to fifty lakh rupees. What did he do with such a huge sum?"

Padma replied, "How would I know? You know that your father always did what he thought was right. He hardly consulted me in all such matters. Besides, I never interfered in all these."

Sridhar intended to ask her something more but didn't know how to go ahead. The thought created a commotion in his head but didn't find a let out. Sambhabana was not to be trifled with. She gazed at her husband frequently indicating that he should go ahead with the questions troubling them. On the other hand, Sridhar felt as if something constricted him and he was not able to speak. This time, she looked at him curtly. Words emerged from his mouth. He said, "Mother! I think we should ask father, before he passes away, where he has parked the entire amount."

Padmabati felt startled. She said, "No question of that. How can we even think of something like that when he is lying on the deathbed? He may take offence."

"You are our only child."

"We don't even have a niece or nephew. I am sure your father must have saved all his wealth for you."

A simple and innocent Padma failed to gauge the storm that raged in the minds of two selfish and devious minds. Sambhabana realized that her mother-in-law was only giving them a cold comfort. She spoke in a harsh and gruffy voice:

"Mother! You have to take the problem seriously."

"We must know what father did with so much money. We have to ask him about it."

"Where has he parked it?"

"Who has he given it to?"

"…or whether he has deposited the amount in a bank?"

Padmabati was disenchanted with Sambhabana for long. She accused the bride from Jajpur of having changed her son. She was about to express her displeasure with the latter when the face of her husband flashed before her. She felt as if her husband was once again repeating to her, "Why do you consider Sambhabana your daughter-in-law?

Consider her your daughter. Only then all your problems will be resolved. You will experience no heartburn"

Bringing her vexation under control she said, "Had he been your father instead of being your father-in-law, would you have asked him on his deathbed where he had parked the sale proceeds?"

Sambhabana spoke unfeelingly as before:

"Yes, I would have surely asked him."

"How would someone know where the money has gone or where it is parked, after he passes away?"

Sridhar supported Sambhabana. He said, "Sambhabana is right, mom."

"In the opinion of the doctors, father's days are numbered."

"I think, you should ask father the details before he breathes his last."

Padma hardly expected such heartlessness from her son. Sambhabana was an outsider; she had entered their family only after marriage. She would somehow accept her unkind words. But, how would she put up with her only son's harshness?" With tears welling up in her eyes, she got up and went away from there.

Sambhabana gazed at Sridhar for a moment. With her mother-in-law in mind, she said, "I doubt this mischievous old lady. I am sure she is only pretending innocence."

"She knows everything and therefore, does not want to have a discussion with the old man."

"She is only giving us a cold comfort."

Pretending that he was not listening to Sambhabana, Sridhar looked into the face of his mother, perhaps to gauge if she was telling the truth or a dark lie.

Fourteen

Throughout the night that day, Sridhar and Sambhabana indulged in closed-door consultations with each other. They finally came to the conclusion that before leaving for London they would dispose of the Bhubaneswar property. They perused the documents and came to know that the house was registered in Padmabati's name. They thought they should rather sell it as soon as possible; otherwise, the old lady might deal with the property in any way she wished, just as her husband had done with the property in the village. The disturbing thought kept them awake all night.

Sambhabana got up at two to collect some water from the fridge. She saw that her father-in-law was deep in sleep. Her mother-in-law kept something securely in a trunk before locking it. She placed the key in a bunch hanging from her waist. The demon of selfishness had already started engulfingSambhabana. She failed to delve into an innocent person's heart. She grew suspicious. She thought her mother-in-law must have stored the entire sale proceeds as well as her ornaments in that trunk. She narrated to her husband what she had seen and what she suspected. Sridhar believed her blindly. Sambhabana's words swept him away just as the swift river currents sweep away a leaf. The semblance of love he had for his mother had a premature death. It was replaced by disdain for her.

Fifteen

Sridhar and Sambhabana got up very late the next morning. Unlike other days, they neither went to Pranakrushna's chamber nor wished him good morning. Just as the *chataka* bird eagerly waits for raindrops to fall from heaven, similarly Pranakrushna waited for his children to wish him good morning and good night. The last time Dr. Senapati had examined Pranakrushna, he forewarned that he was going to live for another fifteen to twenty days. This was already the seventeenth day.

Pranakrushna's voice sounded repressed. He seemed to have grown weaker. His face looked dull and drab. His eyes looked watery and had mucus in them. He summoned Sridhar and Sambhabana to his presence in a weak voice. His voice didn't reach them. Padmabati conveyed to the couple that he wanted to meet them. Both of them were now compelled to come to his presence. Pranakrushna looked at them with weak eyes. He called out to Riya in a feeble voice. Sridhar looked at Sambhabana. Perhaps he read something in her face. He now spoke in a gentle voice:

"Father, Riya is only a child."

"She may catch infection."

"It's better if she does not come to your room."

Pranakrushna wished to see his granddaughter; he wished to cuddle her affectionately. However, he could not express what he wished. His eyes welled up in tears but no one could see those. Padma however understood quite clearly what went on inside her husband's mind. She wiped her tears with the corners of her saree. Sridhar now spoke to his father:

"Father! Please excuse me for asking this. I had requested mama to ask you but she refused to oblige."

"I think I should ask you."

Pranakrushna's body had lost its vigour but his ears were still sharp. While lying on the deathbed, he was able to understand what was happening at home. He remained mum for some time. His silence was torturing Sambhabana. Standing beside Sridhar, she was inciting him to go ahead.

Sridhar spoke a little louder: "Father, what did you do with the money that you got from selling the landed property?"

Pranakrushna heard distinctly what his son was saying but he preferred to remain silent. His face appeared solemn. He didn't expect such a question from Sridhar. The sights of the orphanage flashed before his eyes. The desperate cries of a helpless orphan rang in his ears. How greatly the innocent child of that day had changed! His soul restrained his thoughts. He was after all their only child. Padma could read the feelings of her husband clearly. She spoke in a gentle voice.

"Kanha, listen to me."

"Your father is feeling hurt. Please don't pester him anymore with your questions."

Sambhabana flew into a rage at this. Retorting angrily, she said, "Why don't you disclose it, then? Where have you kept all the money?"

Padma broke into sobs. In an utterly grief-stricken voice she said, "Had I been your mother and not your mother-in-law, would you have spoken like this?"

Sambhabana was getting ready to answer her back. Sridhar pulled her away to his bedroom. They behaved as if they had done a favour to their old parents by arriving from London. In fact, their desire for wealth and greed for their share had brought them there.

Sridhar and Sambhabana spent no time in preparing the Power of Attorney of the Bhubaneswar property in consultation with an advocate. They contacted a few builders so that the property could be disposed of early. On hearing this, Padmabati wailed bitterly. She felt hurt. Even, Pranakrushna didn't know how to console her. He thought of consoling her with, "Please accept Sambhabana as your daughter and not as your daughter-in-law. Do parents ever feel hurt by what their children say?" He didn't wish to say even this much to Padma this time.

While sobbing bitterly Padma said, "Do you now see how Sambhabana behaves?"

"Can you blame me now saying that I treat her as the daughter-in-law and not my daughter?"

"Had she been my daughter would she have dared to speak like this?"

Pranakrushna tried to change sides and gaze into Padma's face. He wished to wipe her innocent tears. He wished to caress her fondly and pat her affectionately for the long years of her love and faith and lighten her sorrows. However, he failed in his efforts. With some effort he called out:

"Padma...Padma."

Padmabati went near him. She whispered into her husband's ears:

"Why don't you reveal what your children demand to know. Why are you making them sad?"

Pranakrushna indicated her to come closer. Padma went near him and brought her ears close to his mouth. She thought her husband was going to reveal where he had kept the money. He however didn't say anything of that sort. He heaved a deep sigh and spoke in an emotional whisper,

"Please pardon me, Padma. I have not been truthful and honest to you."

Padma looked flabbergasted. What could it be that compelled a simple-minded person like Pranakrushna to play false with her? She was left gazing into his face in wonder.

Pranakrushna was waiting for an opportune moment to lay bare his heart. He gave the opinion of others a damn. He gesticulated at Padma to come closer and whispered something into her ears. The moment the revelation was made, he breathed his last. His soul left his physical body. The throbbing of his heart gradually died down, before extinguishing completely. The physical remains lay inert and lifeless.

The revelation caused immense pain to Padma. She

stood by the dead body of her husband, dumb-struck. Hardly a word emerged from her mouth. She leaned against the wall by the bed and gazed vacantly at the ceiling. Before losing consciousness, she was busy thinking how her husband could become so heartless in his treatment to her.

Sixteen

Pin-drop silence reigned in the room. The two occupants lay motionless and still like idols of wood. Chaini entered the room. He called out to his sister-in-law a couple of times but met with no response. Worried, he fetched some water and sprinkled it on her face. Padmabati got up as if from deep sleep. She felt as if she had got up after days of deep slumber. Chaini placed his fingers near Pranakrushna's nostrils to feel his breath. He felt his pulse and cried out in distress, "Sister-in-law, it seems brother has left us."

Padmabati nodded her head to indicate 'yes'. She realized that her husband had kept the secret carefully wrapped in his heart. Once the cat was out of the bag, his life lost its purpose. His dead body was carried to Puri for cremation at Swargadwara. The other rituals associated with death were observed as per custom. A disconsolate Padmabati behaved as if she had become dumb. She hardly offered any opinion but preferred to remain silent most of the time. When compelled to give some reply, she would come up with a brief 'yes' or 'no'.

By the time the rituals were over, the property at Bhubaneswar had been disposed of. Padmabati put her signature wherever Sridhar demanded. She never wished to go through the documents. The property fetched Sridhar fifty lakh rupees. He got the entire amount transferred to his London account. Padma hardly bothered about what he did with the money. She had decided to obey the advice of her husband and to treat Sambhabana not as her daughter-in-law but as her daughter. She also decided not to take their hurtful words to heart. She would rather spend the rest of her life with them.

Exactly on the fifteenth day after Pranakrushna had departed, Sridhar and Sambhabana started packing their bags for their return. Sridhar said, "Mama, pack your bags."

Padmabati knew well that the Bhubaneswar house had been sold off. There was no property left either at Bhubaneswar or their village which she could call her own. She was ready to go wherever her son and daughter-in-law led her, even to London. She stuffed a few sarees and Pranakrushna's photo into an old bag. She also dragged the locked tin box to the portico. Moments later, a taxi screeched to a halt in front of the house. Sambhabana sat on the front seat. She took her daughter in her lap. Padmabati watched till all the luggage was carefully carried to the car. She paid her obeisance at the foot of the sacred tulsi plant. She pressed her head against the wall of the house—the house that was a fond remembrance of her husband; the house where she had spent her days in his company, in a manner of paying tribute. She took a little soil and smeared her forehead with it. She sat to Sridhar's left. Sambhabana was displaying her displeasure again and again as they were getting late. The moment Padma took her seat, she ordered the driver to move on.

Seventeen

The car moved ahead with Sridhar guiding the driver. Padma was feeling disconcerted inside. The fond and cherished memories of the past kept on pathetically flashing before her eyes. She felt as if someone had dropped her into a tub of hot water. The thoughts had blurred her vision and made her absentminded. After some time, the car pulled up in front of a two-storeyed building by a deserted street some distance away from Sundarpada. Many old men and old women stood waiting on the balcony and in the portico to accord them a warm welcome. Sridhar said, "Mama, please get down."

Unable to decipher anything, Padma gazed at Sridhar. Sridhar cast his eyes downwards. Without saying a word, she got down and looked at the building. On a signboard in front of the building, she found the words "P.K OLD AGE HOME" written in big, bold letters. Padma now understood the import of everything. She felt as if her heart was filled with desperate sobs. She experienced wild tremors. She desperately tried to control her breathing so as to calm down. She didn't wish to shed tears lest those drops should turn a curse for Sridhar.

What strange stuff was Padmabati made of? Never ever did she think even for a moment how that orphaned child, whom she had provided shelter and nurtured with love and affection, thought of deserting her when she needed him the most.

Not only Padma but also Pranakrushna was a bounteous stream of such magnanimity. God had made them a shade different from others.

Padma walked towards the portico, followed by Sridhar. Sambhabana however preferred to continue sitting in the car. She ordered the driver to leave the old bag in the portico. The driver was about to carry the trunk, she asked him to leave it in the car. She suspected that the old lady had stuffed all the money that she had got from the sale of their property in the village in it and therefore, she had locked it. She had decided to carry the trunk with her. She was sure that Padmabati would never demand the trunk to be handed over to her.

Sridhar stood by Padma in the portico. The driver left the hand-bag near her. Sridhar said, "I have made arrangements for your stay here. I am sure you will live happily."

Padma stood there like a stone-idol. Sridhar returned to the car. Sambhabana motioned to the driver to move. The vehicle left the place. Padma stood helplessly with her gaze fixed on the car receding from sight. She no longer wished to get the trunk from the car. She had heard Sambhabana say that she had surely stuffed all the money there in it. She wanted that truth should come to light and Sambhabana's ill feelings towards her should be erased once and for all. She had already lost control over many sweet memories that had sustained her so long; she lost the last of those with the trunk. Now, she had no cherished memories to boast of. The old age home was her last resort.

Eighteen

Sambhabana and Sridhar returned to London. They were delighted to have got respite from their responsibilities. Sambhabana had carried the tin trunk with her to London. She thought it must be wrapped in wonder and it could open up vast treasure. After reaching London, she broke open the lock to unravel its mystery. Sridhar joined her. The trunk contained Sridhar's birthday photoswith congratulatory messages written on each of them. She took out the photos one by one. At the sight of those, the couple burst out to laughter. They failed to visualize Padma's emotions and love for her son. To the couple, she was nothing but a silly, useless, countrywoman. After all the photographs were taken out, the couple discovered a yellow dress and a silver locket wrapped carefully in a newspaper. These articles represented the history of Sridhar's childhood. To Padma, they meant a lot.How would the couple understand all these? They rather felt disappointed as their secret hope of getting a large amount of cash had been shattered. Sambhabana held the dress close to Sridhar's body, burst out to a laugh and said, "Take this dress. How fondly your mother has preserved it for you. This will fit you perfectly once you grow old." Both Sambhabana and Sridhar burst out to a loud guffaw.

No one knew why God created such heartless and unfeeling people who crossed all limits of decency. Their displeasure with Padma and Pranakrushna knew no limits as they had failed to get a single penny from the sale of their village property.

Nineteen

God has created women with a greater ability to endure pain. Besides, they can adjust gracefully to all circumstances. She takes birth in her parents' house, grows up there, and turns the place heaven-like. After marriage, she settles down in the house of a person who is a complete stranger until then. She grows acquaintance with the members of that family and sets up a family of her own. Padma was now in her third home—the old age home where she was housed. She had acclimatized to the new surroundings quite well. She would pay obeisance to her dead husband by bowing down before his photo once each in the morning and in the evening. She participated in almost all activities there. The inhabitants adored her. The owner of the old age home came to know about her from the manager. During a visit the owner met Padma in her room. He realized that as a person she was much better than what he had heard about her. He was surprised to see the photo hanging on one of the walls. He enquired about Pranakrushna and his family.

He asked Padma, "Did Mr. Pranakrushna ever talk to you about one Joseph Albert Ekka?"

Padma answered briefly, "Yes. He did. In fact, most often than not, he lavished praise on Mr. Ekka. A very noble and humane person, Mr. Ekka revered my husband as a teacher."

The owner of the old age home spoke in a soft and solemn voice, "Mr. Joseph Albert was not the only noble human being. Mr. Pranakrushna was an incarnation of nobility."

While Mr. Ekka spoke thus, his eyes were brimming with tears. Vigorous sobs constricted him. Streams of tear ran down his cheeks.

Padmabati stood amazed and gaping and listened to the praise heaped on her husband. Unable to check her surprise, she asked, "Sir, how do you know my husband?"

In a sobbing voice he replied, "Mam, I am the self-same Joseph Albert Ekka that your husband often talked about. I manage this old age home."

Since that day, no one addressed Padmabati by her name. They called her 'madam' instead. Even Mr. Joseph called her madam.

Selfless service, sacrifice and dedication endeared Padmabati to every inhabitant. The hapless old men as well as the innocent young children—all of them addressed her by the term 'mother'. It's true that she had been abandoned and deserted but she became a fountain of love for the destitutes who lived there.

The first death anniversary of Pranakrushna neared. The ritual *panda* was to be offered for the salvation of his soul. How would Sambhabana and Sridhar understand the value of ritualistic practices. When Padmabati spoke to Sridhar about it, he simply laughed it out. He said, "Mother, the world has changed."

"No one observes death anniversaries here in London."

"Don't the souls attain salvation?"

"This is just a useless practice."

"Should you need any money, please inform me so that I can arrange to send in time."

A disappointed Padma put the receiver down. However, she didn't allow their words to crumble her. She decided that she would leave for the holy town of Puri, organize a *shradh* and offer food to some brahmins there. With the plan fixed in mind, she waited with bated breath for the day to arrive.

The much-awaited day was only five days away when Mr. Joseph arrived one evening. He went to Padma's room and said, "Mam, I have decided that the first death anniversary of Pranakrushna will be organized here in the old age home. Special lunch will be served to all inhabitants that day too."

"You will be happy to know that Sambhabana and Sridhar are also reaching from London to participate in the celebrations."

Padma felt too overjoyed to respond. A strange joy spread through her veins. The thought of making such grand arrangements for the death anniversary of her husband was beyond her dreams. So much respect, so much adulation! She was indebted to Mr. Joseph for the display of his love for her husband.

On the other hand, Sridhar and Sambhabana were dancing in joy. Earlier they had no idea as to where

Pranakrushna had parked the money that he had got from the sale of all his paternal property. They had now got address of that hidden treasure. Chaini uncle had passed them wrong information. The sale of the property had fetched Pranakrushna not forty or fifty but a huge eighty lakh rupees. The entire amount was parked with Mr. Joseph. Joseph wanted to return them the entire amount.

Sridhar double-checked the sender's address before announcing to Sambhabana, "Do you know dear, why Mr. Joseph has invited us to the old age home where mother is residing these days."

Laying bare her displeasure, Sambhabana spoke in her usual discourteous and harsh voice: "I knew the old lady had deftly planned everything. She had full knowledge of where the money was parked but she only feigned ignorance."

"Perhaps she wants to take the help of Mr. Joseph and go for a division. Don't ever agree with a fifty-fifty plan. Demand the entire amount. We can send her some money every month towards her expenses."

Sridhar usually acceded to Sambhabana's words. He hardly had a personal opinion to offer. He said, "Yes, we need a lot of money to buy a house in London. What's the need of forgoing a justful claim and going for a bigger loan? Don't worry. I'll certainly demand the entire amount."

Twenty

The entire old age home was bustling with activity on the first death anniversary of Pranakrushna. Sridhar and Sambhabana reached the home in time. They were surprised to see the freshly-painted signboard put up in front of the home. The words P.K Old Age Home were replaced with Pranakrushna Old Age Home. Unable to decipher anything, both of them looked at each other, confusedly. The inhabitants of the home accorded them a warm welcome and ushered them inside. A grandly decorated stage welcomed them. A huge portrait of Pranakrushna was placed on one side of the stage. It was gorgeously decorated with garlands. Four chairs had been placed on the stage. Padmabati occupied one of them while Joseph Albert sat on another. The other two chairs were lying empty. The space in front of the stage was occupied by the inhabitants of the old age home and the children's home. At the sight of Sambhabana and Sridhar, Padmabati felt delighted. Mr. Joseph invited them to the stage and offered them the two chairs. The couple wondered why so much love and affection was being showered by the authorities on them as well as on their deceased father. After they settled down, Mr. Joseph went to the microphone. He started narrating his experiences:

"Friends, today is the first death anniversary of Mr. Pranakrushna. He was very simple in his manners and appearance but in reality, he was an exceptional person. His sacrifices, his penchant for serving the poor and the downtrodden, and his love and affection for the suffering humanity placed him on a higher pedestal. On numerous occasions in the past, I bowed down before his greatness. Today, on this special occasion, I wish to narrate before you an incident related to the life of that noble soul.

Everything that Joseph Albert was speaking about Pranakrushna appeared novel not only to Padmabati but also to Sambhabana and Sridhar. They listened to the speaker with rapt attention. Mr. Joseph continued:

I first met Mr. Pranakrushna at this orphanage. With the passage of time our friendship deepened. He would contribute about half of his monthly salary to the orphanage. For eleven years after his marriage, he didn't father a child. I remember a particular incident that happened about thirty years ago. It was the night of Janmasthami. It rained incessantly throughout the night. Hearing the shrill cries of a child, I got up at about two o' clock. On the verandah of the home, I discovered a one-year-old baby boy, dressed in yellow dresses. He had a silver locket of Lord Hanuman around his neck. I didn't want the child to grow as an orphan. I asked Mr. Pranakrushna to meet me immediately. When he did, I handed over the child to him.

For the first time in her life, Padmabati was getting some information about when and where Sridhar was born. Never ever once in the past had her husband told her anything about it. She was wondering as to how she spent such a long time with such a person. Sridhar, on hearing what Mr. Joseph had to say, was feeling ashamed. He was looking helplessly at Sambhabana again and again. He didn't have the courage to look into her mother's face. The yellow clothes and the silver locket that they had salvaged from that tin trunk bore testimony to what Mr. Joseph was saying. He felt as if those lifeless inert objects were bombarding him with shouts of 'orphan,' 'orphan' in his ears. He felt very small. What would Sambhabana feel about him? How would she accept an orphan like him? Wouldn't she make fun of him?

With tears brimming in his eyes, Mr. Joseph continued:

"After two years of the first incident, Mr. Pranakrushna arrived at the home one night. It was midnight. He carried a newborn baby girl with him. His eyes were loaded with tears. His heart was writhing in pain. The baby girl was his child. Mrs. Padmabati had borne the child in the hospital. Pranakrushna was worried that she might start neglecting the boy. Her love and affection for the boy might dwindle. The boy might once again become an orphan. When Padmabati was lying unconscious in the hospital, he took the child with him and rushed to me. She didn't even have an inkling of what had happened. The purpose of his doing this was to ensure the orphan a safe, secure and certain future. I prohibited him from doing it but he didn't listen to me. He requested me to promise in the name of Jesus Christ never to reveal the truth to any one.I promised him not to turn that girl child an orphan. I handed her over to a noble person."

The eyes of everyone present had become moist. Sridhar and Sambhabana were left thunder-struck. Unrestrained tears continued flowing from Padmabati's eyes. Mr. Joseph continued,

"He was associated with the weal and woe of the orphanage. He never forgot to provide regular donations. One day, he disposed of all the parental property in his village and handed over eighty lakh rupees to me. He wanted me to run an old age home with that money. He wanted a veil of secrecy on everything.

He could control his sobs no more. Pointing at Sridhar he said, "The orphaned child of those days has become a Software Engineer. He works in London. He is none other than Mr. Sridhar Kar."

The congregation looked at Sridhar. Padmabati moved towards the dais. The audience clapped for her. Mr. Joseph left the dais to her and moved aside. She joined her palms in salutation and started her address.

"I never knew so many things about my husband. Like all of you present here, I came to know about him from Me. Joseph. He would always advise me to treat my daughter-in-law as my own daughter. I had tried many times but failed miserably. I thought she could never become a good daughter-in-law. Moments before death, he unraveled the greatest mystery concerning us all. "Just remember dear. You never gave birth to a still-born child. You gave birth to a live girl-child. The child is none other than Sambhabana."

She could speak no more. She covered her face with her saree and sobbed bitterly. Sambhabana wished to embrace her and cry her heart out but where from she would gather so much courage! She bent her head down in shame and cried. Sridhar stood mum. He cowered like a culprit and shed tears. He cursed himself for all the misery that he had caused to such noble souls. How could he, who was saved from leading the life of an orphan and nurtured with love and care, dream of rendering the compassionate and beneficent souls orphaned? The moment he shut his eyelids, the voice of his soul reverberated in his ears. It was calling out ORPHAN...ORPHAN.

□□

INCARNATION

One

Piyush and Manashi share a live-in relationship these days. Both of them are software engineers. They live inan apartment in Bangalore. They met at KIIT Collegewhile pursuing engineering degrees and fell in love with each other instantly. Soon, they crossed all boundaries in love. Manashi has been known for her modern outlook since childhood. Her parents belong to the elite classes and are quite modern in their outlook. Her father is an Income tax officer and her mother,a bank manager. The couple owns a palatial building in the posh Sahidnagar locality of Bhubaneswar. Both the parents take great delight in attending clubs and parties.Wine and cigaretteshave become a part of their daily life. They have only one child, Manashi. She has no inhibitions in sitting down with her parents and sharing a drink or a cigarette. Manashi has grown up amidst great affluence and abundant freedom. Taking advantage of it, she had taken a few steps more, selected a boyfriend for herself and settled into a live-in relationship. Not only that, she had not hesitated to abort her foetus a couple of times during the last two years.

She was pregnant once again.

Piyush and Manashi are poles apart. Piyush belongs to the lower-middle classes. A simple country lad, he is a native of Siala Village in Krushnaprasad block of Puri district. His father, Madan Dalei, is a U.P School teacher. His mother, Suhashini, is a house-wife. His father's educational qualification reads M.E. ET. In other words, he had completed his Minor school education. The weal and woe that normally affects the lives of lower middle classes, took their family into its grips too. Piyush is the only son of his parents. Contrary to the wishes of his father, he wasn't selected for admission into a government engineering college. In order to realize the dream of making his son an engineer,his father disposed of the landed property and mango grove that he had inherited from his forefathers and got him admitted into KIIT. Piyush's grandfather had left for his heavenly abode. The old toothless lady, Piyush's grandmother, cautioned her son, Madan several times not to dispose of the ancestral property but he didn't pay any heed. His only dream was to see his son as an engineer. He also wanted him to be settled abroad. If Piyush made a man of himself, it would cause him immense delight. What value did the landed property and the mango grove have in comparison? He dreamt of procuring a building in the city and spending the sunset years of his life there. Piyush shared the dream of his father. He agreed to his father's decision and joined KIIT College. Despite facing great hardships, Madan ensured that his son's wants were fulfilled on demand. Piyush lived like the scion of a wealthy family. From the very first year in the college, he had hooked Manashi as his girlfriend. Within these three or four years, he has learnt how to give her company in smoking and drinking. Like wine and cigarettes, Manashi has become an obsession with him. Now, he finds it difficult to live without her.

Piyush knows very well that Manashi is a carefree and happy-go-lucky girl, who believes in letting bygones be bygones. Terms like pregnancy or abortion hardly distress her. She behaves as if her womb is a lifeless machine that can be switched on and off at will. It can be used whenever she desires and then washed clean. Why should one be bothered about unworthy considerations like humanity or sensitivity? No emotions or regrets ever cloud her mind. All she craves for is sensual pleasure.

While sipping coffee from a mug in one hand and smoking a cigarette from the other that morning, Manashi spoke nonchalantly, "Piyush! Do you hear? I'm pregnant once again."

Piyush's face was initially flushed with unbound joy. In a moment, his joy disappeared into thin air. His face was soon enveloped by dark clouds of despair and desperation. He gazed at Manashi expectantly, while keeping perfectly mum. He marked no change of expression on her face. He was vexed with her. He knew going pregnant wasn't a symbol of love for her; this was only an outcome of momentary excitement. For her, the foetus in her womb was nothing better than a blob of blood or lump of flesh. This was only a stain that needed to be washed clean and done away with.

Blowing smoke out of her mouth in a casual manner, she gazed at Piyush. He had his eyes fixed on her. In a freewheeling manner she blurted out, "Why are you gazing at me like that? Do you see me for the first time?"

Piyush continued gazing at her. He was silent, still and confounded. His teary eyes were saying something but not a word emerged through his lips. Continuing her casual manner, Manashi said, "Are you a philosopher or a lover?"

"Are you in love with me?"

A few drops of tear rolled down his cheeks and fell on the ground. What a cruel, harsh and heartless girl this Manashi was! After sharing intimate relationship with him for such a long time, how she was asking her, "Are you in love with me?" "I have been in love with her since the day I first met her. Each palpitation of my heart repeats her name. Even when I shut my eyes, I find her in my mind's eye. When would this careless girl understand that Piyush isn't enticed by the attraction of her body? He loves her; he's deeply attached to her; he can't live without her."

At the sight of tears welling up in Piyush's eyes, Manashi fell silent for some time. The expressions on her face underwent a change. She appeared solemn, extinguished the cigarette and deposited it into the ashtray. She coolly looked into Piyush's eyes and flashed a smile. She said:

"Emotion! What the hell this emotion is all about?"

"Let's go to the clinic, wash it off and get it all over."

"No emotions, no tensions."

Piyush broke his silence and sighed heavily. He became intensely emotional and said, "Manashi. This is exactly why I'm tensed."

Manashi didn't really understand what was going on in Piyush's mind. This wasn't the first time she was talking about pregnancy or abortion. This had happened many times earlier. Every time that happened, Piyush himself accompanied her to the clinic as her husband. Never ever in the past he had become emotional or worried. Manashi spoke as if she didn't really comprehend what the matter was.

"What's the real cause of your tension?"

"Is it my pregnancy?"

"No." retorted Piyush.

After a brief pause he said, "We are fully aware of what's happening. We're mature adults.."

"What do you want to say, then? Manashi asked.

Piyush found it difficult to express his true feelings to Manashi. How would he tell her he wasn't in favour of another abortion? Even though they maintained an intimate relationship, he didn't know whether Manashi really loved him or not. From the very first day she had cautioned him not to construe their relationship as anything more than mere friendship. Their relationship was only a means of killing time. Her parents would never accept Piyush as her husband. Therefore, he should never place the proposal for marriage before them. Piyush had agreed to the proposal and accepted her offer of friendship.

Piyush agreed to her proposal but on the very first day, he fell in love with her. He didn't want to lose her. So, he restrained his heart and mind and agreed to all proposals floated by her. His love for Manashi had grown into a weakness. Life without her was inconceivable for him. His heart and his breathing uttered her name. Sadly, he dared not express his feelings to her. How would he say that he wished to marry her; that he wished to show the child in her womb the light of the day; and that he wished to embrace him as father?

Two

Everything in this world needn't be expressed through words; even though unstated, certain things are explicitly understood.

Manashi wasn't a kid. Besides, she had been sharing live-in relationship with Piyush for the last three years. At times, she perceived his weakness for her but she would deliberately put on a veil of ignorance. She acted as if she hardly knew a character named Piyush. Although he didn't express his emotions overtly, his manners, countenance and eyes spoke volumes about that. She had a thorough understanding of what he wished to convey. She understood that Piyush loved her and wished to make her his own, forever. At times, she would think of taking their relationship seriously. This change had come upon her after going through two abortions. However, every time the process of abortion was over, she would soon forget all about her promise. She would be lost in dreams of a fresh bout of excitements and a gorgeous future.

Perhaps her understanding of Piyush was getting deeper now. She had grown careful in her treatment of him. Piyush was waiting for the change to take root in her. In an emotional voice he said:

"Manashi! Can't you manage without going for abortion?"

Manashi feigned as if she had understood nothing and said, "What do you mean?"

Piyush blurted out in an emotion-charged voice:

"We would show him the light of the day. We would bring him to the world with promises of a better future.'

Manashi burst out to a laugh. That day, however, drops of tear rolled down her cheeks. She was able to restrain the grief she experienced but the tears would obey no restrictions. In a manner of issuing a warning, she told Piyush:"What do you mean by 'we'? Have you forgotten the conditions we had set at the beginning?"

Gazing downwards, Piyush spoke in almost a whisper:

"Yes! I remember everything. But, can't we make amends?"

"But why should I?" Manashi blurted out. Piyush looked into her face. He wasn't crying; he didn't appear crestfallen either. He had garnered enough courage to face the truth. His face had lit up; his eyes were glistening. He laid bare his heart:

"Simply because I love you."

"The 'love' I am talking about didn't germinate in a day. It has been there since the day I saw you for the first time. Since the day I agreed to your proposal, I have been seething on the funeral pyre of sorrows. I am certain, one day or the other I am going to lose you. That would be the last day of my life, for sure. I have no alternative other than waiting helplessly for that day."

Tears had welled up in Piyush's eyes. Manashi seemed concerned about him. How wouldn't she be? Did she bear a heart of iron or steel? She was made of flesh and blood. How cruel could she be and for how long? She decided to fight with her parents for Piyush's sake. She could never allow his love for her to die an untimely death. If needed, she would fight with a tiger. She would surely become a mother and give birth to the child growing in her womb. Both of them would show it the light of the day. Manashi's heart throbbed with affection. She was transformed into a devoted, affectionate and compassionate woman as well as a loving mother. She hugged Piyush and kissed him on his forehead. Piyush was taken by surprise by her sudden change in behavior. He felt flabbergasted. He dreamed as if he had grown huge wings and he flew around the earth in a few minutes. He was eagerly waiting for such a moment for long. He had never imagined that his dream would come true and Manashi would fall in love with him. It was perhaps the most cherished moment of his life. He gazed at her with his eyes wide open. His heart was ready to burst but not a single word emerged through his lips. Silent though, he was busy fashioning a world for himself and Manashi.

Manashi broke the silence first and said:

"No one can separate me from you, Piyush. "

Piyush was waiting to hear this much from her. Before she could finish, he dragged her towards him and gave her a tight hug.

Three

Emotion influenced Manashi's judgment and choice. Without weighing the pros and cons of the matter, she took a huge decision concerning her life. The moment the thoughts of her parents invaded her mind, she found herself in deep distress. A mountain of confusions stood blocking her path. Throughout the night, sleep eluded her. With a cup of coffee in one hand and a cigarette in the other, she prepared herself to confront the world. Doubts assailed her mind. How could she discuss the matter with her father? She would rather discuss it with her mother. The dilemma persisted for a few days. One day, she gathered courage and rang up her mother. Although they talked over five minutes, she dared not bring up the topic for discussion. She hardly realized what to say and where to start. What should she talk about first? Her being in love or about the live-in relationship!

She didn't wish to disappoint Piyush any longer. She finally Whatsapped her mother, "Mom, I'm pregnant".

The message startled Mousumi. A shiver ran down her spine. She read it repeatedly. She checked the sender's phone number. She was confirmed that the message had in fact come from Manashi's phone. Without any delay, she rang her up. Manashi had prepared herself for the situation.

She picked up the receiver and waited silently to hear her mother's reaction.

Her mother's rude and disconcerted voice reverberated in her ear:

"What nonsense? What's the fun all about?"

Manashi remained silent and pocketed the abuse. Her silence was making her mother restless. Her doubts about her daughter's misdemeanor were getting confirmed. The intensity of the abuse deepened. Manasi spoke only once:

"I...I'm pregnant."

Mousumi felt as if the world beneath her feet had collapsed. Unable to decide how to respond, she remained mum. Manashi was her only daughter. She always ensured that Manashi grew up amidst affluence. There was no doubt that her outlook was modern. They had also allowed her enough freedom. However, they had never thought that she would cross all limits like this. She found it impossible to continue the conversation and hung up.

Manashi wanted that her mother should be angry with her; she should scold her, but she should talk with her. Her mother's silence worried her. What would she do now? How would she convince her? Feeling utterly helpless and desperate, she waited for her mother's call. After some time she received a message that her parents were reaching Bangalore by the evening flight. She felt bewildered. Time hung heavily on her. Anxiety-ridden, she roamed about the rooms. She had to face the storms boldly and remain firm in her decision. She informed Piyush about their arrival. Piyush shifted to a friend's flat for the night. Deeply confused, she was lost in thoughts of how to face her parents.

Four

Manashi looked down from the balcony of her flat. A taxi halted in front of her apartment. The sound of its horns broke her reverie.Her mother, Mousumi, and father, Manas Samantray, arrived at the appointed hour. Manashi said 'Hi, Dad,' 'Hi Mom' to lend them a welcome but they had gone completely irresponsive. They weren't happy with what Manashi had done. How could they be? They prided themselves in being called modern but how they could side with their only daughter who had taken such drastic steps. Manas babu sat down on the drawing room sofa with a thud. He took out a cigarette from his pocket and lighted it. Mousumi dragged Manashi by her hand and entered the bedroom. She took out a prega-kit from her handbag and said, "I want immediate confirmation."

Manashi gazed into her mother's face. The sight of her flushed and fuming face prohibited her from registering any protest. She entered the bathroom with the prega-kit. She returned to show it to her mother. Mousumi planted a tight slap on her cheek. Tears welled up in Manashi's eyes but she remained mum. In a rude voice she asked, "How many months?"

Manashi spoke gently and with patience, "Three plus."

Mousumi planted another slap on her cheek. Perhaps she raised her hands on her for the first time. She didn't remember when the last time she had punished her. Perhaps when she was a child! Without any further delay she suggested, "Let's get it aborted. It's already late. There may be complications if we delay any further."

Manashi had prepared herself mentally for this situation. She was well aware of her mother's attitude. She remained silent. After a moment, she nodded her head to say 'No'.

Mousumi yelled, "But why?"

"This is not the first time. I have aborted at least twice earlier."

Mousumi gazed at Manashi in utter disbelief. She experienced a great deal of heartburn. Manashi's behavior compelled her to wonder, "Is it the same child I had given birth to?" Manashi spoke vehemently, "I have decided not to abort anymore."

Incensed, Mousumi said, "Since when have you grown up to take decisions about yourself?"

"I'm in love," said Manashi after a brief silence. Mousumi gazed at her with wide open eyes. In a "There is a limit to love. Love doesn't mean to fall pregnant. Do you know how the society treats girls like you?"She said gruffly.

In a manner of losing her cool, Manashi retorted, "How? I give it a damn."

Mousumi roared in anger, "You idiot! You want to hear it from me. Aren't you ashamed of yourself?"

Mousumi felt flushed in anger. What would she tell her? What language would she use to scold her? She was searching for the proper definition of being 'modern' in the present society. She wondered if she had committed a mistake in infusing modern values in Manashi. Was it what it meant to be 'modern'? She had not dreamt, even in her wildest dreams, that being 'modern' could prove so disastrous. Perhaps Manashi had readied herself mentally to marry Piyush. She had referred to him many times during their conversations since their student days. Mousumi knew very well that he was her best friend. But how she would guess that meaning of 'best friend' was this. Her attention was drawn towards some jeans trousers and t-shirts. Mousumi asked, "Whose are these?"

"All these belong to Piyush. We share a live-in relationship." Mousumi felt as if she suddenly crashed from heaven. She had seen such things in television serials. She would feel vexed at those characters. She thought no such thing happened in India. All these were confined to alien cultures. But her own daughter had crossed all limits of decency. Despite being a lady who maintained a modern lifestyle, she wasn't able to savour these. She had lost hope of any amendments too. However, she couldn't resist herself from firing a volley of questions, "Is it a foreign country? What culture is this? How dare you maintain a live-in relationship? Will the society accept you?"

"This is not a village, Mom, this is Bangalore. These days one can find many instances of couples sharing live-in relationship even in Bhubaneswar. Besides, Piyush is my best friend. I love him. We have decided to get married soon."

Mousumi had heard many times about Piyush from Manashi. Every time, she spoke about him as her best friend. Manashi would often say, "Piyush belongs to a poor family. He is a country lad. His family is not so educated and he lives in a remote village. He is worthy of being a companion for a while but not for life. He is extremely simple. So, I adore his friendship." How could this opinion of her change? What would she do now? She hadn't revealed anything to her husband about Manashi's pregnancy. She simply told him that Manashi had severe gynaec ailments. How would she reveal such a shameful thing to him?

Manashi spoke in no uncertain terms, "Listen, Mom! I'm surely going to marry Piyush. Better you decide about your course of action. I know if you agree to the proposal, father won't have any objections. We are adults. We have the right to take decisions concerning our lives. We have already decided what course to follow."

Mousumi gazed at Manashi threateningly with wide open eyes. She was fuming with anger. Although she was silent, her face spoke volumes about her disappointment. She seemed as if she would tear Manashi into pieces. After a moment of silence, Mousumi turned her face away from Manashi. She rushed out of the bedroom and sat down beside her husband on the sofa. Her husband handed her over the cigarette he was smoking. She smoked it in great puffs. She placed the butt in the ashtray. Smoke billowed from the ashtray in spirals. Although she concentrated on the spiraling smoke, her anger showed no signs of abating. What would she tell her husband? How would she tell him such a shameful thing? She suddenly blurted out, "Let's go."

Manas babu was taken by surprise. He said, "Where?"

An exasperated Mousumi said, "Let's go somewhere. I can't stay here another moment.'

"But, Manashi is unwell!"

Mousumi replied, "No, I had lied to you. We'll discuss everything at the hotel. If I linger here anymore, I'll surely turn mad."

Gauging Mousumi's mental condition, Manas babu didn't risk asking any more questions. Both of them reached the hotel. They left for Bhubaneswar by the morning flight.

Five

Manas and Mousumi reached their Bhubaneswar home. No conversations took place between them for quite some time. For two days, Mousumi didn't ring up Manashi. Manashi didn't ring her up either. In fact, she couldn't muster courage to initiate a conversation. An unknown dread enveloped her. What would be her mother's decision? She knew her father wouldn't be able to render any help so long as her mother didn't give a nod. He was extremely meek, a puppet in her mother's hands.

How bold she herself had become! What she dared disclose before her mother, she would never have been able to discuss with her father. By now her father must have become aware of everything--her falling pregnant, her frequent abortions and the probability of her not conceiving again. What would her father be thinking about her? Even though he didn't express his opinions openly, he wasn't a small child. She grew up playing in his lap. She was his darling. How ashamed he must be feeling!

Two days had passed; it was the third day since she had met them. Sorrow and shame must have bent him down.

All of a sudden, the phone rang. Manashi felt irritated. She reached for it. It was her Dad on the other side. She felt nervous. How would she face him? How would she answer his questions? She was undecided about whether to pick up the phone or not. The phone was disconnected while she was dithering about like this. It rang a second time. She picked up the receiver and burst out to a loud wailing, like a small child demanding a chocolate. After shouting 'Hello, hello' a couple of times, Dad went mum for a moment. Then in a calm and gentle voice he was heard consoling her, "Relax…relax dear.'

When Manashi heard her father's soothing and consoling voice, she felt really relaxed. Perhaps her father had pardoned her. However, she continued wailing as before, in recognition of the mistake she had committed. It was as if she regretted for her past actions and repented. Manas babu was heard saying, "I have discussed everything with your mother. You and Piyush are getting married soon. Most probably this month." Manashi stopped wailing, just as a kid does on getting a chocolate. Her surprise knew no bounds. She never even imagined in her wildest dreams that her father would be successful in swaying her mother's opinion in their favour so soon. She felt a little reassured. She thought, "Before disconnecting the phone, father assured me that our marriage would be held by the end of this month. Today is the seventh of the month. It means, I have to wait for another twenty-four days." She conveyed the happy message to Piyush. Utterly surprised, he stood like an idol of stone, gaping. He took the name of God reverently and sought His blessings. The following day he reached Bhubaneswar by flight. He wanted to discuss about the developments with his father. Excitement and anxiety clouded his mind. He left for his village without any further delay.

Six

Piyush's parents lived in their native place, a mofussil village, far away from Bhubaneswar. To be precise, it was situated at a distance of two hundred kilometres from the capital city. The roofs of all houses in the village touched each other. If one wished to reach their house, one had to leave ten houses from the beginning and visit the eleventh one. Theirs was a South-facing house with two rooms at the front. The rooms had asbestos roof. Besides, there was a passage room. At the front, there was a five-foot wide verandah. Originally, the verandah lay at a height of five feet from the road in front. The road was re-laid under the *Pradhanmantri Gram Sadak Yojana*. Now the verandah was left at a height of only two feet from the ground. Piyush's grandmother, the old lady Pakei, would be seen sitting on the verandah most of the time. She had lost all her teeth owing to old age but she had carried the name Pakei meaning 'toothless' from her parents' place. Her villagers knew her by that name since childhood. The old lady rested on the verandah most of the time. Most of her contemporaries had left for their heavenly abode. She was about ninety. Owing to old age, her vision had become blurred. But, she had been endowed with the uncanny ability of identifying a person by the smell of his body and the sound of his footsteps. Her sense of smell was astoundingly sharper than that of an Alsatian dog. If someone enquired what her age was, she would immediately reply, "It would be three or four years less than five scores."

The taxi screeched to a halt in front of their house. The old lady was sitting on the verandah. She jumped to her feet crying, Piyu! Piyu!"

She mumbled happily and muttered something in an inaudible voice. It sounded like the bitter wailings of a village woman. Piyush touched her feet in reverence. She hugged him. She could never keep anything under the veil of secrecy. She whispered into his ears, "A new member is arriving very soon."

Piyush couldn't get what she was hinting at. He hardly gave it a damn and entered inside. Besides the two rooms at the front, there was a row of four rooms on the eastern side. One of those was used as the bedroom of his parents. In another one, the farmhand lived. The last two rooms were used to store paddy and ragi. The kitchen stood at the end of all rooms. Irrespective of whether it rained or a storm blew, the verandah in front of the kitchen was used for the purposes of dining. The latrine was constructed about a hundred feet away from the rooms. Piyush insisted on his father to construct one, only two years ago. He stood on the verandah and hollered, "Bou! Bou!"

There was no reply. His mother, Suhasini, had perhaps left to take bath in the village pond. After some time his father, Madan Dalai, appeared and stood at a distance from Piyush. Piyush reached him and touched his feet. He shouted for his mother once again, "Bou! Bou!"

Piyush's grandmother was found reaching the courtyard. She said, "Why are you shouting? I told you just now, a guest is coming to our house very soon."

Not only today, never ever in the past Piyush gave her a damn. However, Piyush's father rightly guessed what the old lady was hinting at. He frantically gestured to her to fall silent. As he failed in his endeavor, he said, "Silence… silence.'

Then he gave Piyush a weird look and stood like a statue. It was as if he was meeting Piyush for the first time in his life.

Piyush was in a great hurry. He wished to convey his decision to both of his parents as soon as possible and return to Bhubaneswar. His marriage was going to be held there. It was not possible on the part of his father and mother-in-law to set foot in this mofussil village. The taxi waited for him outside. Manashi was found ringing up to him frequently and enquiring, "When did you reach there? When are you coming back? What happened there? Is everything Ok?"

He felt more comfortable in the company of his mother. He could divulge the details of his love-affair and the impending marriage the following week only to his mother. His mother was a great support in his life. He didn't dare tell his father that he had already taken such a huge decision, that too without consulting him. Irrespective of his education and his earnings, how he could talk shamelessly about all these things before his father. His father was after all a teacher. He had taught him the first lessons in A, B, C, D…

Desperate, he called out again, "Bou! Bou!"

Looking in the direction of his old grandmother he said, "Grandma! Why don't you tell where mother has gone?"

The old lady felt a little vexed and said, "Do you ever listen to me? Why should I waste my energy? I have been talking about a great news. Do you bother to listen to me?"

A restless Piyush blurted out, "I know what the grand news is. I have come to convey it to everyone here."

Madan babu felt a little comforted. The old lady stood gaping. Her eyes were left wide open. She thought, "How could he get a hint of what was going to happen? How did the matter get leaked when a veil of secrecy was put on it for more than four months? Which idiot leaked the matter to him? Oh! These children of the new generation; they can easily outsmart anyone."

At this time, Suhasini reached from the pond, carrying some utensils in her hand. At the sight of her, Piyush fondly called out, "Bou...Bou." He rushed towards her, carried the utensils himself, and kept them on the verandah. He hugged her and said, "Bou! You have put on much weight during the last two years."

Suhasini stood mum like a stone-pillar, unable to decipher how to react. Piyush was her only child. She had prayed to and worshipped Gods to gift her with another child but the Gods hadn't granted her wish then. She wished to bear a girl-child but in vain. The old lady Pakei had a clear understanding of the unsavoury situation that had been created. She shouted at Piyush:

"Piyu! Why are you acting smart when you say that you know everything? Your mother has conceived again. She is four months into her pregnancy. Wouldn't she appear a little bloated?"

Piyush stood thunder-struck. He stepped away from his mother as if she was a strange person. He cast a disdainful look at his mother, returned the gaze, and looked at his father. His father bent down his head in shame. Next, he looked at the old lady, Pakei. He shouted:

"You contemptuous witch! Were you hinting at this since then? Why didn't you reveal everything up straightaway? I would have gone away without meeting them. You are responsible for all this."

By then he was seething in anger. Manashi called him up exactly then. He didn't know how to respond to her. In anger, he hurled the phone on to the ground. The phone broke into pieces. The taxi was waiting at the door. He took it and left for Bhubaneswar.

Tears breached all barriers and flowed in gushes. She rested her hand on her tummy and gave out a loud wailing. She felt as if she was an impious sinner. She had committed a grave sin by bearing another child. Because of this, she had lost her courage to face anyone.

Seven

After Piyush had departed, Suhasini and Madan felt like lifeless logs. Madan sat leaning against the wall and gaped at the outstretching vast sky. He felt as if he would go crazy. He could visualize the moon shining during the day and moths flying in front of his eyes. He was little concerned about what people would say at school when they learnt that his wife had conceived at such an age. He was disconcerted at the fact that his only son derided them. He felt guilty even to see his own reflection in the mirror. He despised himself; he scorned at what he had done.

The old lady Pakei had never before seen her son and daughter-in-law in such a desperate state. Streams of tear ran down from her eyes. She comforted her daughter-in-law and fondly caressed her. While caressing her tummy she said, "Don't feel disheartened. You carry happiness in your womb. You can see God in its innocent smiles. Even, an enemy can't turn his face away from it. At the sight of its enchanting face, your sorrows and tears will disappear. Have patience only for five months."

Sorrow and shame made Madan angry. He said:

"What's the worth of your consoling words when things have fallen off the precipice? I was ready to go for abortion. However, you insisted on her keeping it, saying that we must honour the god's gift. This time a girl would be born. She would be an incarnation of Goddess Lakshmi. Her birth would usher in joy. Do you now see what joy has been ushered in? The little happiness we enjoyed has left us forever."

Madan sir broke into violent sobs, like a child. His mother found it difficult to endure his pain. The old lady caressed his head fondly and wiped his tears. She comforted him. She said:

"My dear! My jewel! Don't cry my child. Don't feel sad. Children are the blessings of God. After Piyush was born, I had insisted with my daughter-in-law to go for another child. One eye can't present a complete view; one child can't complete the family. The family which doesn't have a daughter isn't worth much. Didn't we pray Gods years ago to bless the family with a daughter? God has granted you the boon…albeit a little late."

The old lady continued consoling his son for quite some time. Unable to restrain his anger, Madan blurted out, "To hell with the boon! Your God hasn't bestowed a blessing on me; He has rather snatched away all pleasures. I am going to become a father at a time when my son should become one. You are the root cause of all troubles."

Seething in anger, he left the place. He submitted an application for leave to his headmaster that very day. He procured grocery items for the old lady; he made all arrangements for her. He packed his bag and baggage and left for Bhubaneswar with his wife. While they were leaving home, the old lady beseeched him to let her know what the matter was and where they were heading.

Madan babu paid her no heed. While leaving home, he told her:

"Listen, mother! I feel crestfallen. These aren't streams of tears but blood flowing from my eyes. I earnestly request you not to discuss anything with anyone. Put yourself under some restraint. If someone enquires about us, please dispose them of by saying that we have left on a tour."

The old lady grimaced and sat down with a thud. She guessed it rightly that her joys were going to be short-lived. She silently cursed Piyush for all the trouble. Everything was heading in the right direction; the sudden arrival of the boy smashed all hopes. She earnestly prayed to God to return her joys. Her eyes welled up in tears. It seemed as if the old lady and not Suhasini was writhing in pain. Not tears but blood streamed from her eyes.

Eight

A disconcerted Piyush left his village. He felt as if he the world had suddenly gone topsy-turvy. The taxi reached Bhubaneswar. He stayed with his friend. He had lost his hunger, thirst and sleep. He felt orphaned. What would he inform Manashi? What would she think when she knew about all these? What decisions would she take? He felt dumbfounded. He visualized a huge snare laid in front of him and felt as if he had been caught in it. No escape was possible from it. He could only writhe in pain and cry in distress. He couldn't muster courage to call up Manashi.

When Piyush was a child, he was proud that his father was a U.P school teacher. When he was admitted in the same school, his ideas about his father underwent some change. He learnt there was a difference of heaven and earth between M.E, C.T and M.A., B.Ed. When he left Parikuda to join the S.C.S. College for higher studies, he realized how poor his father was. By the time he was admitted into KIIT, the idea had stuck to his mind that they were 'very poor fellows'. Now those parents and that old lady were all as good as dead for him. In this vast world, he was left with no one whom he could call his own. For the last five days, he had been drinking bottles after bottles of wine. His friends had no idea of what troubled him; he didn't disclose what ailed him either. They all thought he must have fought with his girl-friend. The issue would be resolved in a couple of days. Although a week had elapsed, no solution was visible.

Manashi felt desperate when her repeated calls went unanswered. She was not one to wait in patience for seven days. She thought perhaps Piyush had deserted her. He wouldn't return. She wore bangles, put on the vermilion mark, and started for the clinic. She requested the doctor to go for abortion. Since she was a regular there, the doctor had no objections. He asked her, "Where is your husband these days?" Manashi felt a little baffled. She didn't know what to say. It suddenly came out of her mouth, "He's in Dubai."

After a brief pause the doctor said, "You see! There is some complicacy this time. I think both of you should take the decision together. If you abort this time, you'll be left with a very faint possibility of conceiving again."

Manashi felt startled. Her head reeled. She was reminded of her parents. She felt as if she had grown orphaned. At the thought of her future, she felt distressed. Darkness enveloped her mind. She returned to Bhubaneswar by flight that day itself. At the sight of her, her parents grew surprised. Without saying a single word, she shut herself in her bedroom. She sent a number of messages to Piyush's cell phone. Under the prevailing circumstances, she needed his support badly. Life without Piyush was inconceivable. All she wanted was Piyush—not her parents' support, not their houses or landed property, and not even property worth crores in and around Bhubaneswar.

Mousumi thought Manashi and Piyush must have quarreled with each other. Not Piyush but Manashi must be at fault. She knew her and her stubborn character. She tried to take advantage of the situation. Manashi hardly shared the secrets with her father or mother. She waited expectantly, like the Jacobin cuckoo does for raindrops, for Piyush to ring up. Sleep eluded her. She had never waited for someone's call so expectantly. She writhed in pain and wriggled like the fish caught in the fisherman's net. She had used Piyush initially as a friend and then as a playboy. Finally, she fell in love with him. Now she found him as the father of her last child growing in her womb. She perceived the importance of Piyush. She now understood quite clearly that a husband was not needed only for the fulfillment of physical hunger; he was rather a wife's soul. He was like her life-breath. She decided that she would give birth to the child growing in her womb and show her the light of the day. If needed, she would wait for Piyush till her last breath.

Nine

After almost ten days, Piyush's voice from an unknown number startled Manashi. She couldn't prepare herself mentally to answer Piyush, who was shouting 'Hello... hello' into the phone. She felt breathless. After some time, she faintly replied, "Hello'.

Piyush sobbed like a child. Manashi also sobbed. She could realize his helplessness from the bitterness of his wailings. She asked, "Piyush! Tell me what has happened."

Manashi knew Piyush very well. He could never deceive her. He darenot do that. Piyush's helplessness made her forget all her sorrows. He didn't reply to her questions but went on crying.

Moments later, both of them met each other on the coffee lawns of Hotel Marrion. Whilelost in an intimate embrace, both of them tried to control their tears. Fortunately, all other tables were lying empty that day. Manashi silently listened while Piyush narrated all the details of that day.

Manashi was born and brought up in the city. Her schooling, college education and job—everything was attained in the city. She had grown up in a small family. It consisted of her father, mother and herself. She never met her paternal grandfather and grandmother. When she was in standard three, her maternal grandfather and grandmother passed away in quick succession. They were also inhabitants of Bhubaneswar. They belonged to the upper classes. Her maternal grandfather was an I.A.S. officer whereas her paternal grandfather was an I.P.S officer. How could she understand the affairs and emotions associated with village life? How would she comprehend the love and affection of Piyush's parents and the immense faith that the old lady Pakei placed in God? She only comprehended that Piyush's mother was pregnant. He had left home after a tiff with his parents. He refused to have any relationship with them. He felt orphaned and helpless. She also comprehended that Piyush's family was hundred times less educated than what she had conceived of them. Very poor and uneducated! She treated them not only with disdain but rather with pity. Without giving the troubles a damn she told Piyush, "Take it easy. Cool down. Don't be serious or feel let down at all. Why do you think you have become orphaned? I am with you. I carry our child in my womb."

Manashi's statement made Piyush feel light at heart. He felt like hugging her and planting kisses on her forehead. He restrained himself thinking that he was on the lawns of a hotel. However, the tears rolled down unhindered. Manashi's transformation surprised him. He experienced a flood of love and affection in him for her.

Manashi rang up to her mother and said, "Mom! Proceed with the date you had scheduled for our marriage. It's only five days away. Piyush and I are in Hotel Marrion at the moment. A new problem has cropped up. None from his family is going to attend the marriage."

Piyush had never known Manashi could talk so

audaciously with her mother. He was surprised. Once someone takes a firm decision and resolves to go ahead with it, no matter what obstacles bar his way, he is bound to taste success. He gathers immense courage, equivalent to the strength of a hundred lions, to face the adversities. Manashi had become an incarnation of such undaunted courage. She was like a pregnant cow; protection of her child was her only concern.

Mousumi ridiculed when she came to learn about the absence of Piyush's family. She said, "What do they think of themselves? Do they match us in wealth and regard in the society? How dare they refuse to attend the marriage? It's their good luck that we have agreed to the proposal."

Manashi lost her cool and quipped, "It's nothing like the way you think. Piyush's mom has just conceived."

Mousumi yelled loudly into the phone at this. Manashi thought perhaps a bomb had exploded near her ear. She had guessed her mother's reaction was going to be like this. Mousumi continued roaring like a wounded tigress. Manashi had fallen completely silent. She continued holding the phone to her ear for about ten minutes like that. Finally, she turned it off. In great anxiety and dilemma Piyush asked, "What happened? What did Mom say?"

Manashi replied, "Do you expect something better to happen? We are getting married today. Just look outside. There's the Ram Mandir. I have been rendered an orphan just like you. But I don't want to render the child growing in my womb an orphan."

This is exactly how things shaped up. The same day, both of them got married at the Ram Mandir. The following day, the couple returned to Bangalore. With the live-in relationship turning history, another significant phase commenced—a phase of intense love and caring.

Ten

Through an acquaintance, Madan took a small house on rent in the Sundarpada area of the city. The couple lived there. It's true that they were living under the same roof but they hardly displayed any concern for each other. They were concerned only about Piyush. Thoughts like what he would be doing, how he would be living, what he would be thinking overshadowed their minds. Both of them writhed in immense pain. Madan often wished to ring up his son but he couldn't muster courage. Besides, he didn't have Piyush's new number with him. Piyush had discarded the old number and damaged the SIM just as he had shunned all relationship with his parents and old grandmother.

Suhasini didn't display any concern for the child growing in her womb. She prayed to God most of the time, "O God! The doctor failed to abort the child growing in my womb. Please abort it somehow." Madan harbored similar thoughts. He sincerely wished that a dead child should be born to him. However, he couldn't express his feelings to Suhasini; how could he? She was after all a mother. She carried the child in her womb and gave it life through her blood. How would she wish death for the child herself? They silently bore the wishes within themselves without giving them expression. Strangely, the relationship between husband and wife had turned a curse, a sin. They were both facing the consequences of that sin. They had reached the city so that the fruit of that sin could be detached from the tree and discarded by the roadside. If a still-born child was born to them, their job would become easy and they wouldn't have to indulge in sin.

The old lady Pakei sat on the front verandah and shed tears. She earnestly prayed to God for the safety of her Khusi. Though old, she loved children. At the sight of a small child, she would feel joyous. Her soul danced in joy whenever her eyes fell on a girl-child. Since the day Piyush had grown up, no child's voices reverberated in their house. No child played in their courtyard. She always prayed to God to bless her child with a daughter. How would she accept when the question of annihilation of the child surfaced? She counted the months. As the date of delivery neared, her desperation grew manifold. Her heart writhed in pain at the thought of trouble to her dear Khusi. She shed drops of blood instead of tears from her eyes.

Eleven

Piyush and Manashi have gone on leave these days. They have decorated their Bangalore flat like a doll showroom. They have been eagerly waiting to welcome the newborn baby. Manashi had not even dreamt that Piyush loved her so deeply. She had never seen her father taking so much care of her mother. The experiences of the last five or six months made her believe that she and Piyush had been playing the role of husband and wife of some elegant story. At times she wondered if she was in a dream. On some other occasion she would think if there were husbands like Piyush in this world. What care! What love! What concern he displayed for her! Now she realized that she wasn't just in the treatment she had meted out to him. He was a rare breed. It was from him that Manashi learnt how to love someone. She didn't wish to allow thoughts of anyone except Piyush and her child entering her mind. Days passed by. The expectant couple lived happily.

Finally, the appointed day arrived. As per advice of the doctor, Piyush admitted Manashi into Apollo Hospital at Bangalore for child-birth.

The day Manashi was admitted into Apollo Hospital, Suhasini was experiencing severe labour pain at their residence in Bhubaneswar. Madan tried his best to soothe her pain. He was found telling her repeatedly, "Try a little harder. Push a little harder. If the child is born here, no one would have an inkling of the matter. We can easily discard the child into a bush and return to our village."

Suhasini heard nothing. She was writhing in intense pain. Without even opening her mouth and uttering a word, she was squirming in pain. She was praying to God. She thought God was punishing her for her sin. There was not even an iota of love and affection for the child. Suddenly, Madan found that Suhasini was no more able to withstand pain. He dreaded that things might turn disastrous if he delayed any further in shifting her to a hospital. He didn't take any risk any further. He admitted her in a nursing home nearby.

The old lady Pakei was praying to God. Strange are the ways of God. He blessed one family with two babies. For one, he ensured divine pleasures even before he was born. For the other, life was no less stinking than that of a worm. How strange is the dispensation of God! However, the old lady Pakei hadn't lost her faith in God.

Twelve

The doctors were taking great care of Manashi in Apollo Hospital. All of a sudden, her condition deteriorated. The doctor said, "The case has suddenly grown complicated. It'll be difficult to ensure survival of both the baby and the mother."

Piyush requested the doctors not to disclose anything to Manashi. He had heard from her that it was going to be her last child. She could never become a mother after that. He felt restless and forlorn. He sat on a bench lying in one corner of the hospital and cried helplessly like a child. After some time, she rang up his mother-in-law. This was his first call to her. He had hardly any relation with them since their marriage. The words of Piyush left Mousumi shell-shocked. Manashi was after all their only child. Forgetting all anger and disappointments, the couple reached that night at Apollo Hospital in Bangalore. By then the doctors were pressing hard for a quick decision. "Please take a decision within fifteen minutes as to whom we should save. Otherwise, both the mother and the baby will be in peril."

Mousumi found herself facing a great dilemma. She and her husband knew it quite well that Manashi would never be able to become a mother ever again. Piyush brought their attention to the fact again. Mousumi kept gazing both at her husband and Piyush in great bewilderment. There was hardly any time left to ponder over things. They found it difficult to take an immediate decision. Manas said, "We don't have a heir. At least the child has our blood. We need the child to survive."

Mousumi didn't say anything in reply, although she found it difficult to fathom her husband's views. She was found eagerly looking at Piyush waiting for him to make a quick decision. This time the doctor emerged from the operation theatre and said, "What decision have you taken?" Without giving a damn to others' opinion, Piyush cried out, "I want Manashi, doctor. I want her only. I can't live without her."

Mousumi looked at Piyush in wonder. Neither sorrow nor regret tainted her face. It was true that her husband owned immense wealth, an elitist attitude, and great name and fame but he didn't possess a compassionate heart like Piyush. She reached the conclusion that Manashi was very lucky to have him as husband. She loathed her husband.

The doctor emerged from the theatre and said, "Manashi is all right. Sorry, we couldn't save the baby-girl."

Even though his heart was enveloped in immense pain and sorrow, Piyush felt relaxed at the thought of Manashi. Mousumi wished to comfort Piyush but her sense of pride and ego prevented her.

Thirteen

Sorrows never abandon the distressed. They follow man like his shadow. Madan and Suhasini had been swimming in the sea of sorrow for long. After going through immense pain throughout the day, Suhasini had a normal delivery. Oh! What a divine looking child it was! Fair complexion, chubby cheeks, sharp eyes like a deer's, long and pointed nose like a needle, blood red lips! The baby-girl looked like the idol of goddess Lakshmi. Even an adversary would appreciate her beauty. The nurse said, "What name have you chosen for your baby?"

The name suddenly emerged from Madan's mouth, "Khusi."

Suhasini was left gaping. With wide open eyes, she gave her husband a surprised look. She was thinking of her old mother-in-law. It was as if she had been speaking through Madan's mouth. Tears welled up in her eyes. She was concerned about the child and its future.

Suhasini was discharged from the Nursing Home after two days. The earlier plan of abandoning Khusi near some bush had already been erased from their mind. They searched for an orphanage, left Khusi there, and started for their village. The conscience of the couple was pricked by thorns with every step they took towards home after leaving Khusi in the orphanage. They had considered the child a sin; they had hated it from the core of their heart. Now the smiling face of the child weaved a magic sweeping them off their feet. They were travelling physically, true but they had left their minds and hearts at the orphanage. Concern for the society dragged them physically towards their village but the attraction for Khusi caused an opposite pull. They hardly remembered how they reached the Baramunda Bus stand, how they took the bus to their village, and when the bus stopped at the village bus stop. They were jolted out of slumber when the conductor was heard shouting, "Madan Sir! We've reached your village stop. Won't you get down? The bus has to leave."

The husband-wife duo got down. They hired an auto -rickshaw. It stopped in front of their house. The old lady Pakei burst out to a wailing at the sight of them. However, her eyes were directed at Suhasini's lap. The intensity of her wailing deepened at the sight of her empty lap. Madan put his hand on the old lady's mouth and took her inside. The news of their arrival soon spread throughout the village. The village women arrived one by one. Madan was compelled to speak up. He whispered into Pakei's ears, "A still-born child was delivered. I had to discard it there."

The village women and neighbours left one by one. News about the still-born child spread like wild fire in the village. The old lady found the entire thing difficult to digest. She prayed to God regularly; she had immense faith in Him. She shed tears for Khusi.

Fourteen

Madan joined school after a few days. How long would he remain absent from it dreading backlash? He felt bashful at first. His male and female colleagues often hurled double entendresat him. The offending words would enter one ear to escape through the other. He hardly cared how they criticized. Khusi's face would often flash before his eyes. Her attractive eyes, sharp face, pointed nose, and charming smile floated before his eyes. Every moment he cursed himself for his inhuman act. He failed to pardon himself for flinging an innocent child into a sorrowful, agonizing, and uncertain future. Suhasini suffered profound agony like her husband. She found it difficult to walk with her head held high. She would grow absentminded and bump into things often. She would have no knowledge even if blood oozed out of her body. The old lady Pakei cautioned her several times. She had to call in the local doctor and get the wounds bandaged. Suhasini had gone crazy in a matter of few days. She had almost turned dumb. If someone asked him four or five questions, she would answer once with a 'yes' or 'no'. She had lost her control on her tears; they flowed in gushes, unabated.

Can growing age diminish mother's love and affection? Irrespective of the age at which a woman embraces motherhood, her love and affection for the child remains the same. How could Suhasini release herself from Khusi's attraction so early? Despite the best of her efforts, she failed miserably. Love for children is a special feeling. Even an animal can't detach itself from it; how could Suhasini have done so? She was a human being after all.

Fifteen

Manashi was discharged from the hospital in due course and returned to her flat. Manas babu and Mousumi returned to Bhubaneswar in a couple of days. Like a sky overcast with dark, rain-bearing clouds, their minds were enveloped by a sense of despair. A feeling of desperation and hopelessness permeated throughout the day and night. The condition of Piyush and Manashi was worse than the condition of Manas and Mousumi at Bhubaneswar. Piyush tried her best to make Manashi happy. Was 'happiness' a fruit that Piyush could procure from the market? Money can buy pleasure, but such pleasure is fleeting. A basketful of 'real pleasure' lay lurking in man's mind. He who knows how to unlock the basket, can have an access to unbound pleasure. Piyush tried his best to help Manashi unlock the basket but in vain.

Manashi and Piyush went to bed after dinner. Suddenly Manashi said, "Piyush, I find it difficult to put up with the cartloads of dolls, teddies, and cartoons lying in the room."

Piyush responded softly, "It's Okay. I'll think of what to do with them later. Have you taken your medicines? You must take rest. The more rest you get the better. Please don't cloud your mind with ominous thoughts."

Manashi had in fact not opened her heart before her

husband. The loads of dolls and teddies reminded her of her child. They also reminded her of her unrestrained lifestyle and frequent abortions. They yelled into her ears she could never become a mother in future. How would she share all these with Piyush? She tried to lie on bed silently. Sleep eluded her. Under the effect of a sedative, she fell asleep at about three.

Since she went to bed late, she got up late. She sighed deeply. She threw a glance around the room. She could hardly believe what she found. There was not a single doll, teddy or cartoon anywhere in the room. Even no portraits of children hung on the walls. The walls were adorned with Manashi's photos. A few of Piyush's photos were also there. The bedside table had a huge bouquet of roses on it. She washed her face and cast a look around the passage, drawing room and dining space. Their look had undergone a transformation in a single night. She looked at Piyush in eyes of wonder. He presented her a rose and wished her 'good morning'.

Manashi had thought perhaps Piyush wouldn't be able to decipher what went on inside her mind. To her surprise he said, "No one will disturb you today onwards. Only you and I will live here. You are my world." Manashi looked into Piyush's face in eyes of wonder. How self-centred she had been all the time! She had used Piyush for physical pleasures. She wanted to dispose him off like a cigarette butt. How great that person was! How deeply he loved her! Despite the knowledge of the fact that she could never become a mother, there was no decline in his love. He wished to shower all his love on her. This thought made her feel joyous. She thought, "I am undoubtedly one of the most fortunate girls in this world."

Sixteen

Although Manashi had recovered physically, she felt mentally unstable. She couldn't excuse herself for the mistakes of the past. She found that Piyush was never concerned about himself; he was only concerned about Manashi and her happiness. He worked day in and day out to bring her joy. Joy to Manashi brought him pleasure. Manashi had witnessed Piyush's sacrifice and love for a long time. At times, she encountered his inner pain and despondence. Had Piyush really forgotten his parents and the old lady Pakei? 'No way'. Piyush had a large heart. His heart was an ocean of love, affection and genial feelings. He could never forget the love and affection of his parents so easily. She felt it was not good to be selfish and ignore his inner suffering. At times she felt guilty herself. She thought she had treated Piyush and his family coldly.

One day Manashi told Piyush, "Piyush, I am not feeling well. I want to spend a few days in the lap of nature, far away from this city and this house."

Piyush jumped in joy. He felt as if Manashi had guessed what was going on in his mind. For the last few days, he was thinking of taking her to a hill station on holiday. Besides, Manashi had a fascination for places like Ooty and Kodaikanal. During their Bangalore stay, they had visited Ooty on numerous occasions and Kodaikanal on a few others. Piyush said, "I was planning for a visit to Ooty or Kodaikanal."

Manashi said, "No! Let's go to an extremely interior village and stay there for a couple of days."

Piyush responded, "In that case, Kerala will be a better option. Let me make arrangements. We shall start tomorrow."

Manasi said, "The village I have in my mind is not in Kerala. I'm talking about a beautiful islet of my dreams. The village would be situated on that islet. On one side of it, there would be the vast outstretching waters of Chilika Lake and on the other, the endless ocean. On the edge of the village, the wavelets would be dancing. There would be the astounding congregation of exotic birds and the symphony of their chorus. Where would one get all these!"

While she was a student of KIIT College, she had heard many times Piyush describing the beauty of his village. The emotion in the description made her feel that he must be in love with the grand sights and sounds of his village.

Piyush had a vision of his parents and the old grandmother, Pakei. An intensely emotional person, he had tears welling up in his eyes. Within moments, the two eyes were brimming with tears. Before the tears ran down, he took out his handkerchief and wiped those away.

He said, "I have snapped all relationships with my past life. I don't wish to remind myself of those."

Manasi said, "Piyush! In the past, it was your village

and your address. Now, it's our village and our address. If you forget, I'm there to remind you."

In a soft and gentle voice, Piyush explained, "You better forget about it."

Manashi had always been headstrong. Once she took a decision, she would never listen to anyone. In a manner of fueling an argument, she said, "What do you mean?"

Piyush said, "I have told you about my parents. Do you think the step taken by them was correct? Can they show their face to anyone in the society? Even I can't show my face to anyone in the entire Parikuda area. They are uneducated. They aren't ashamed of themselves. Before indulging in such sinful acts, they should have thought deeply many times."

Manashi was looking at Piyush with sharp eyes. She had undergone strange transformation over the last few days. She was no more a girl; she had grown into a woman. She had become an ideal wife and a concerned daughter-in-law. Like an ideal woman she argued, "Which act of theirs do you brand as sin? Mother-in-law hasn't committed any sins. What they have done is their right. They have obtained license from the society to indulge in such acts. Whatever we were indulging in for such a long time was a sin. Our relationship was illegitimate. To live in a room without marriage and share a live-in relationship was a sin. Going for frequent abortions was a sin. You never considered our actions as sinful. Why? Had my mother-in-law or father-in-law been involved in extramarital affairs that would have been illegitimate or sinful. Before pointing your finger at them, please evaluate your actions once. Just have a look at the illegitimate life we led. Who should be branded uneducated- they or we?

Piyush was looking at Manashi for a long time. Was it the same Manashi who frowned at the prospect of visiting their village? She addressed the villagers as uneducated and rustic fools. He was surprised to witness the transformation in her. He thought, "I'm really fortunate to have got one like Manashi as my life partner. How mature she is! How deep her understanding is! Wonderful."

Piyush now spoke in a calm and soothing voice, "Manashi! Will Mom accept your views?" Manashi spoke rudely, "Piyush, Mom might have been kind to you but not to your parents. She is an adamant, proud and self-centred person. They have held on to their ego. I know how mother reacted when I informed her about mother-in-law's pregnancy. Mom visits night clubs and attends whole-night parties. During those, wives are exchanged. No one objects to that. Isn't that a sin? Forget about the society. Forget about Mom. A loving and caring person like you needn't take permission from a heartless person like her. I don't expect such courtesy from you."

Piyush was listening to Manashi, dumbfounded. At times, he was found swallowing spittle. He was able to visualize his village, his parents and the old grandmother, Pakei. Manashi said, "Piyush! We have established certain relationships after coming to the world. Some other relationships have been established by God. If you wish, you can get many Manashis, many mother-in-laws but there is no second mother. You may get many father-in-laws but you have only one father. And the old lady Pakei is like God. How long will you live without them?"

This time, Piyush no longer took the help of the handkerchief. The tears rolled down in gushes. He hugged Manashi and wailed bitterly like a kid. It was as if the Bay of Bengal of his heart was lying dormant, and it suddenly turned violent and its waves rushed shorewards. He thought he would go to his village; he would go back to his parents and the old lady, Pakei. He would request them to pardon him. To make amends, he would lie in their laps, like Lord Vishnu lying in His divine posture.

Seventeen

Preparations were made to leave for Piyush's village. Both of them reached Bhubaneswar. Piyush collected information about the village, parents and home from his friends. They stayed at Bhubaneswar for about eight to ten days. One morning they took a hired taxi and started for their village. As they moved forward, Piyush started narrating the beauty of his village. Manashi had heard the descriptions many times. She now had the opportunity to witness the reality. She thought, "Piyush doesn't possess adequate knowledge of the Odia language. The beauty of Lake Chilika far surpasses the beauty that he had described." She was amazed at what she witnessed. The lake that spread on both sides of the road and the continuous chirping of the birds all along enchanted her.

As the taxi approached his village, Piyush's excitement inflated. He felt as if he hadn't paid a visit to his village for many years. The road sides, the *Kasatandi* groves, and all starting from the cattle to the villagers, appeared novel. How novel an experience separation can cause! When the roar of the sea reached his ears, he blurted out, "Manashi! Can you hear the roar of the sea? Our village is situated only at a distance of half a mile from here. Our village is close to the estuary, where the river meets the sea."

Manashi was smiling faintly, witnessing the joy,

intimacy and emotions of Piyush at the sight of his village. This was what she had desired in him—an abundance of joy and happiness. When he felt enraptured, she felt a secret sense of satisfaction in her.

The taxi entered the village. On both sides of the road, houses stood in lines, with their roofs touching each other. The houses stood ten hands away from the road. Piyush's house was next to ten houses from the entrance to the village. Smile disappeared from Piyush's face the moment the taxi entered the village. His face appeared solemn and grim now. His eyes turned moist. Patting him softly on the back, Manashi said, "Relax! Everything will be set right. Just shut your eyes and say, 'All things shall pass away'. I mumble this when I'm in trouble."

Piyush asked the taxi driver to stop at his door. He looked at the verandah. The old lady Pakei sat there. At the sound of the taxi, she guessed Piyush must have come. She didn't shout 'Piyu...Piyu' this time. Holding on to the wall for support, she entered inside. She went inside her bedroom and shut it. Perhaps her fresh wounds bled at the approach of him. She wailed and shed tears for her Khusi.

Piyush opened the door of the taxi and entered the house like a sinner. He stood on the verandah and looked around. He saw no one in the vicinity. He tried to call out 'Bou,' 'Bou' but felt as if the word stuck to his throat. Perhaps he dare not call her; perhaps no words emerged from it as his penance. He stood on the verandah and wailed like a child. Suhasini emerged from inside. At the sight of Piyush, she felt flabbergasted. She had already turned dumb. Her mother's love for Piyush pulled her towards him. She hugged him and burst out to a loud wailing. Madan emerged from his bedroom and joined the duo in wailing, leaning against the wall. He was still considering himself a sinner.

Piyush touched the feet of his father and lay prostrate on the ground. Madan babu hugged him. The tension in the atmosphere eased a bit. Piyush said, "Please pardon me. I have committed another mistake."

Both of his parents looked in his direction. He said, "I have already got married."

Looking in the direction of the road at front, he called out, "Manashi…Manashi."

Manashi got off the taxi and came in. Pointing at Manashi he said, "This is Manashi, my wife."

He took the baby from her and said, "This is our daughter, Khusi."

Suhasini and Madan felt startled. Manashi touched their feet and sought blessings. Both of them looked at Khusi instead. Suhasini took the child to her lap and felt surprised. The same nose, same eyes, same hair, that round face and the same rosy lips. She planted a number of kisses on her cheeks. She yelled, "This is my Khusi…my Khusi… my Khusi.'

The sound of the wailing penetrated the walls of the old lady's bedroom and reverberated inside. This was followed by the cries of the child. The moment the sound reached the old lady's ears, she lost her patience. She unbolted the door and emerged. Her eyes fell on Khusi. The baby was crying. The old lady ran towards Suhasini and plucked the child from her lap. She sat on the ground and held the child in her lap. Khusi's wailing ceased immediately. It was as if she was waiting for the warmth of the lap of the old lady. The old lady planted innumerable kisses on her cheeks. The child pinched the old lady's nose. All of those who were assembled there looked in the direction of the old lady.

She said, "Who said there's no God?"

"God has many incarnations."

"My Khusi is my God."

"This is my Khusi...my God."

The old lady, Pakei, held the child close to her bosom and shook like leaves in the wind. In the baby, she experienced the existence of divinity. Suhasini, Madan babu, Piyush and Manashi looked at her with their bewildered eyes wide open. They had a glimpse of her deep faith in God and humanity.

The old lady had found her God.

□□

Black Eagle Books

www.blackeaglebooks.org
info@blackeaglebooks.org

Black Eagle Books, an independent publisher, was founded
as a nonprofit organization in April, 2019. It is our mission
to connect and engage the Indian diaspora and the world at
large with the best of works of world literature published
on a collaborative platform, with special emphasis on
foregrounding Contemporary Classics and New Writing.

www.ingramcontent.com/pod-product-compliance
Lightning Source LLC
Chambersburg PA
CBHW050417110726
47899CB00008B/2758